More books by Alan M. Clark,

available in paperback and ebook. Most are also available as audio books

Of Thimble and Threat
The Door that Faced West
Say Anything but Your Prayers
The Surgeon's Mate: A Dismemoir
The Prostitute's Price
A Brutal Chill in August
A Parliament of Crows
Apologies to the Cat's Meat Man
Mudlarks and the Silent Highwayman
Fallen Giants of the Points
The Paint in My Blood: Illustration and Fine Alan M. Clark

Praise for the writing of Alan M. Clark

"Crime and horror wrapped in a wondrous symmetry, made all the more terrifying by its factual basis, *A Parliament of Crows* has it all. Read it!"
—F. Paul Wilson, author of Cold City

"In a publishing landscape where everything has been done...to death, comes something marvelous, frightening, and new—*The Surgeon's Mate: A Dismemoir*. Alan M. Clark has birthed a masterpiece that oscillates between bone-deep confessional and hide-your-eyes-horror."
—Charles Atkins author of *The Prodigys*

"*Of Thimble and Threat* is a terrifically absorbing read. A mature novel and superbly researched. The image of silver in the blood was woven expertly and made the ending luminous and poignant."
—Simon Clark, author of *Vampyrrhic* and *Night of the Triffids*

"Clark proves himself to be the ultimate double-threat, his prose every bit as evocative and compelling as his art. Steeped in Victoriana *Say Anything but Your Prayers* is a worthy edition to Ripperology."
—Steven Savile, author of *Silver* and *London Macabre*

"In *Jack the Ripper Victim Series: The Double Event*, Clark's attention to details of the era reveals a class system where a poor woman alone is all but doomed to an early grave. Readers will come away touched by these profound portraits of desperate women and shocked by not just the crimes which ended in their demise, but the greater crimes of a society that offered them no hope. This book is a must-read; be prepared to be horrified."
—Nancy Kilpatrick
Author: The Power of the Blood series

Editor: *Danse Macabre* and *Expiration Date*

"*The Witch of Wapping* is Dickens made even darker. Though a relatively brief novel, it spans nearly seven decades, and contains multitudes of mystery. Made up of a series of first person narratives, Victorian period documents, and kaleidoscopic points of view, it offers a grim, supernatural puzzle that can be solved only by the reader. The grimy London setting is so perfect that you can taste the soot and dust, the characters are true and compelling despite their darkest motives, and the evil at the story's heart is eerie and haunting. A rich, vicious, and delectable treat, with plenty of bite."

—Chet Williamson, author of *Ash Wednesday* and *Second Chance*

From the review of *A Butal Chill in August* in *Ripperologist Magazine:*
Everything about this novel inspires admiration. It reveals terrible things about the world of London's poor, yet it is a work of great beauty, ceaselessly entertaining and compellingly readable. The rigging of a ship burning in the fire at the London Docks 'sparkles like a spider web dripping with dew at sunrise'. When we finally meet Jack the Ripper, he emerges from the darkness like an ordinary man, smelling of sulphur and soap. *A Brutal Chill in August* is a triumph.

From the review of *Apologies to the Cat's Meat Man* in *Ripperologist Magazine*:
Alan M. Clark is not the first author to find the victims' lives irresistible, but he has no equal when it comes to writing vivid and intellectually provocative stories about them. This is storytelling of the highest quality.

The Will'ven't Bin

a novel by Alan M. Clark

IFD Publishing
P.O. Box 41281, Eugene, Oregon 97404, U.S.A.
www.ifdpublishing.com

The Will'ven't Bin

Cover art, Copyright © 2025 Alan M. Clark

ISBN: 979-8-9931706-0-2

Printed in the United States of America

Acknowledgments

Thanks to Lisa Snellings, Cynthia Drewek, Dave Conover, Randy Fox, Alice Merritt, Margaret R. Clark, William M. Clark, Ethan Evans, aka Esan Ebansu.

Extra thanks to Dave Conover for his suggestion for the cover art and his helpful comments on the characters and plot of the story.

Inspiration for this novel came in part from what my father, William M. Clark, told me of his early life in Nashville, Tennessee.

Examples of Indian relics the author's father and grandfather found in the Nashville, Tennessee area.

The Will'ven't Bin

a novel by Alan M. Clark

IFD
Publishing
Eugene, Oregon

Examples of American Civil War relics the author's father and grandfather found in the Nashville, Tennessee area.

Chapter 1

Following the Great Crash of '29, a lot of down and out folks came to our door to ask for work and food. Mama turned all of them away at first because the decision-making about such things had always belonged to Daddy and he had fallen too ill to do the job. I suppose she thought he'd take all that up again once he felt better. Turned out, he had polio and didn't recover. He died in the fall of 1931. I missed him terribly.

Right after Daddy died, Mama told me, "I expect you to take over many of his responsibilities." She did not mean his decision making. She would be in charge of that. Watching her over time, I decided she didn't make good choices.

Although I did all of what I could, at twelve years of age, there were some of Daddy's responsibilities I wasn't smart enough, large enough, or strong enough to do. And, of course, I didn't control the purse strings.

We lived in the neighborhood of Oak Hill, part of Nashville, Tennessee, a place with people needing work at the time. I picked my battles with care, bugging Mama to hire someone to fix those things we couldn't afford to lose.

"I don't like dealing with strangers," she said.

"Most are honest folks not looking to harm anyone," I told her.

"How would you know? You're just a child."

"Paying homeless people who have no jobs to work doesn't cost much," I said. "Some will settle for being fed in return for their labor."

Grudgingly, she did hire a few people to help out.

In the winter of 1932, the roof needed mending. Mama hired Everett Glass, the black man who did our garbage collection, to put new slate on the roof. The galvanized plumbing had always been a problem. In the spring of 1933, we got little more than a trickle out of the kitchen sink. She hired a plumber named Emil Plumber to replace the pipes. About that time, the electrical switch in the parlor would occasionally spark, and the lights would flicker. Because I worried aloud that the house might catch fire, she'd spoken with our neighbor, Sylvia Westlake, about hiring someone.

"The religious ones are more likely to have a conscience," she told Mama. "I know a man."

Though not a strong believer, herself, Mama had agreed to hire Sylvia's electrician, a man named Theo Pickering.

Thank goodness for Daddy's life insurance. The payout from the policy made all that hiring possible.

I was in school when Pickering came to do the work and didn't meet him.

"Stop that," Mama told me, as I stood in the parlor that evening, turning the light switch on and off and grinning. Whatever she might say, I had gotten her to move.

With a desire to have a driveway for the used automobile she meant to buy from a neighbor, Mama hired again. On a hot day in early August of 1933, Seth Knopes knocked on our door. I got there after he and Mama had begun to talk.

"This is my son, Martin," Mama said, "and this is Mr. Knopes." She gestured.

"Hello," I said.

He didn't quite look at me as he nodded. "Seth, please," he said.

"Now I remember," Mama said. "I've seen you at the A&P. You bag groceries there."

"Not anymore," Seth said, his voice sounding hoarse. "Certain women complained that I looked too unhealthy to be bagging their food."

"They must not know or appreciate that you were harmed fighting for us all," Mama said, shaking her head.

Seth shrugged.

"If you clear that part of the hedge," she said, "I'll pay you five cents an hour. I'm looking for work, myself, so I'll have to leave. Martin will be here if you need anything. You'll have to get all the roots so they don't grow up through the gravel we'll put down."

"Yes, Ma'am, I can do that."

He began to cough. Standing there watching him, doing nothing, I felt foolish. The coughing went on for a while.

Mama also looked uncomfortable. "Let me get you some water," she said, and hurried to the kitchen.

She returned with a glass of water and gave it to Seth. He took a quick sip before a new bout of coughing began. When he'd settled down again, he drank most of the water and handed the glass back to Mama. He wiped his eyes, mouth, and nose with a stained handkerchief.

"Are you sure you're up to the work?" she asked in a kindly manner.

"Yes, ma'am," he said. "Just a quick spell. I have them from time to time. It'll pass shortly."

Seth coughed again, cleared his throat, said, "If you hurry over to the A&P and ask for my old position, you might get it. It's the sort of work and pay teenagers get, but it's a start, the first rung on a ladder. Maybe you shouldn't tell them we spoke."

"I'd feel funny about that, benefitting from your suffering," Mama said.

"Don't. You have to take what you can get these days."

Seth stood at least six feet tall. For reasons unknown to me at the time, he kept his head and eyes facing downward. I took that to mean he hid something from us. From what I could see of his face—mostly the sides of his cheeks and his ears—he looked to have spotty skin and deep lines. Up close, that made him look old, though I would have placed his age at about forty years. His blonde hair had a patchy, mangy look. I saw his scalp peeking through here and there when he took off his flat cap to scratch his head. His clothes were worn out. He smelled of stale tobacco smoke, and like he needed a bath.

I had doubts about the man and couldn't imagine Mama seeing anything religious about him.

Still, she fed him a ham sandwich and a glass of milk, then sent him to the side yard.

Once he'd gone to begin the work, Mama turned to me. "I have to go to the fabric store. Trudy says she'll take my antimacassars on consignment. You play with your dog and stay out of Seth's hair. Help him only if he asks for it. Keep track of how long he works, to the minute if you can. It's now five 'til, so let's say his start time is noon."

I followed her into her room where she loaded a bunch of her handmade lace and tatting into a carpetbag. I knew she'd have to walk two and a half miles along Franklin Pike to get to the fabric store downtown, so she'd be gone a couple of hours at least.

"What about the A&P?" I asked.

"Yes, I'll stop there on my way back."

Somehow, I didn't take her seriously. I didn't think she truly wanted a job.

"Get the pick and shovel from the utility room and take them out to him," Mama said. As I stood dithering, she said, "Go! The clock is ticking." She headed for the door to leave.

My doubts about Seth aside, I'd grown bored. Spending time with him would at least be something new.

Soon as I stepped outside, my German shepherd, Fritz, joined me. I hurried to the utility room, got the tools, and went out to the side yard.

When Seth caught a glimpse of us—me carrying the tools, and Fritz being a dog, I guess—he crouched down like he feared an attack of some sort.

"It's just me," I said.

"And the dog? Is it mean?"

"No. That's Fritz. He wouldn't hurt a fly."

Seth seemed unsure for a moment, and only slowly grew more relaxed.

"Fritz, huh?" he grumbled, then said more under his breath that I couldn't make out.

I placed the shovel and pick on the ground behind Seth.

Fritz came up and licked my hand. I scratched behind his ears, and he leaned into it, his eyes squinted up like he'd never felt anything that good before.

Seth untangled the hedge plants with his hands. He took a big knife from the overstuffed sack he'd tossed onto the lawn and used the blade to cut away much of the greenery. That weapon had what looked like brass knuckles as part of the handle. I'd seen one at the Army/Navy Surplus Store. The clerk there called it a *trench knife* and said that soldiers used them in the Great War.

Though he'd been holding his sack while standing at our front door, I hadn't thought much about it. Now I saw that it was a World War One haversack, much like those Daddy had gotten for us at the Army/Navy Surplus Store.

Had Seth served in the Great War?

I thought of the lead WWI soldiers I played with. Daddy had gotten the molds for me, and I had cast a small army of them. In painting the soldiers, I'd just started using red to give some of them wounds. I hid that from Mama.

Had Seth suffered something in the fight in Europe that left his skin that way? Had he been in a fire or had a German soldier turned a flame thrower on him? His skin didn't look quite like what I'd seen on other burn victims. I had too many questions I couldn't bring myself to ask.

Although Seth kept his head down and I couldn't see his pupils, he seemed to eye me curiously from under his brow as I sat in a shady spot in the grass and watched him work up a sweat. His expressions were lopsided and hard to read, like whatever controlled his face, or at least the right side, had been damaged.

Seeing the top of a bottle of liquor poking through a hole in the haversack, I thought Mama might have spoken the truth when she'd said, "Most of the down and out are drunks, just looking for a handout." Had seeing him working at the A&P made him more deserving in Mama's eyes. I'd always had trouble understanding what made her tick.

Seth took up the shovel, checked its edge with his thumb, and began to dig around the base of the privet hedge plants. Each stump, its roots tangled with those of its neighbors in the old hedgerow, took about an hour to pull. Seth went at the work at an even pace, except for pausing occasionally to cough. While he did sweat a lot, he didn't appear to tire. I had on Mama's homemade bug repellent and didn't think to offer him any. He had a dozen mosquitos going after him and did nothing to ward them off. He simply kept at it, digging and prying the shrubs apart as if angry with them, tearing them from the ground in pieces and throwing them on the lawn.

I hauled it all to the yard trash pile in the northwest corner of our lot. Later, I'd strip the twigs and leaves away to make kindling out of the woody parts.

Returning from the trash pile for another load, I saw Fritz nosing around the edges of the growing dirt pit. Ever curious about what lived in the soil and probably hoping for some fatty grubs to eat, he tried to help Seth, but instead got in the way.

At first, with a glance at me, Seth shooed Fritz away gently. With time, though, he took to cursing at him and then lashing out with a slapping hand against the dog's rump.

"Don't!" I said.

Seth looked up. As if shielding his eyes from the sun, he held a hand up to his brow. Again, his eyes were lost in shadow. Because the sun hung in the sky behind him, I decided he'd used his hand to prevent me from getting a good look at him.

"Why, you're just a boy," Seth said, half his face an ill-tempered mask, the other half expressionless. "You have no business telling *me* what to do."

I turned away, took up a thin stick, and poked at a short mound of dirt that looked like a tiny volcano growing in a bare spot on the lawn. Instead of lava, black ants poured out. Trying to stop them, I stuck the twig into the hole in the top of the mound. They pushed out around it. Some crawled up the stick toward my hand. I dropped it, got up, and moved about ten feet away before sitting again to watch Seth.

Upon hearing the distant, deep thumps and knocking sounds of railcar couplers connecting in the train yard to the southeast, I saw Seth crouch down in the pit and fold his arms over the top of his head. That looked much like what he'd done when he saw Fritz and me earlier. I tried to picture him cowering in the trenches of WWI as artillery shells rained down explosions and shrapnel, something I'd learned about from Daddy and a few friends, yet truly couldn't imagine.

Seth stuttered a few words I couldn't make out. Finally, he looked up and around, and went back to work. After that, if I made a sudden move, he'd glance at me quick, like he had to make certain I wasn't going to do something to harm him.

Me, at 12 years of age?

I tried to think of something funny to say to make him laugh or at least make him smile. No success. I couldn't think of anything.

With time, he grew more relaxed. "I'm sorry for fussing at your dog," he said, his words coming out friendly all of a sudden. "I'm on my own so much, sometimes I don't know how to be with people, or, well, with dogs."

"That's all right. Since school let out for the summer, I don't see many people either."

Silence for a time, except for the sounds of Seth digging, chopping, cutting, and Fritz moving about.

"I seen you playing in the woods across Franklin Pike, and later down by the creek. Are there fish?"

I didn't like the idea that he'd watched me. "No, some minnows, crawfish, and salamanders, that's all." I needed to discourage him from going near my creek, so I added, "Oh, there are snakes and snapping turtles too. Sometimes they come up on the banks and wander around looking for something to bite. My Daddy always said 'If a snapping turtle bites you—"

"Yeah, yeah, '…it won't let go 'til it thunders.'"

"That's right."

He didn't seem alarmed by the idea and I decided that anyone having spent time in the trenches of WWI would not be easily frightened by small animals, even vicious, poisonous ones.

"Do you live close by?"

"Over near Lipscomb College," he said.

I knew that to be about a mile away.

"Seen anything strange in the woods hereabouts?" he asked, "something like a junk yard?"

Still not sure of him, I shrugged. "People dump stuff in the forest all the time, old automobiles, furniture, broken farm equipment, but not all in one spot."

"Surely an adventurous boy like you would know everything about the nearby woods. Why, when I was your age, I knew the woods near home backwards and forwards and had my favorite hunting spots."

I wanted to ask Seth if he looked for something in particular. Instead, for some reason, I asked, "Where did you grow up?"

"We're not talking about me," he said sharply, and spit in the dirt at my feet.

His sudden change of mood startled me. I almost got up to go back in the house.

He stepped up out of the pit in my direction and leaned over so his shadow covered me. I got a deep chill, though the temperature had to be about ninety degrees. "You *will* tell me what you've found hidden in the woods," he said, as if making a threat.

Scooting on my rump to get away from him, I said, "I don't know what you mean."

He backed down and returned to the pit, muttering. "You will tell me, eventually."

I shrugged again, holding my hands palms up so he'd know I had no more to add.

Had he gone mad? Again, I thought about going back in the house.

Seth turned his back to me, stopped talking, and went to work, so I stayed.

On his third stump, he said, "Why don't you go look for some shears to help cut free the smaller roots?"

I went to look in the utility room and didn't find any shears. Seeing the axe, I thought that might work. I had some worry about offering Seth a tool that could be used as a weapon.

Returning with the axe, I saw Fritz trying for something in the dirt near the man. Driving the shovel into the soil with both feet, Seth slipped and fell to one side, landing atop the dog. Fritz let out a cry and scrambled free, leaving the veteran lying on a bunch of sharp, broken roots. That must have hurt.

He stood and stepped out of the pit, his anger showing only on the left side of his face. Could be that confused Fritz, because he cowered down, ears flat, yet didn't run away.

I had little time to think what to do as I got a bad feeling about what would come next. I should have told Fritz to run.

Sure enough, Seth spun on him. "God damn German bitch!" he shouted, and kicked the poor dog in the gut. Fritz let out a yelp and fell gasping to the ground. Seth took up his haversack, and headed for the street.

I dropped the axe, and hurried to help my pal. "You're not a bitch," I said. "You're a good boy." Coughing, Fritz got his feet under him, glanced fearfully in the direction Seth had taken, and slunk away through the privet hedge at the northern edge of the yard. Stupidly, I just watched him go.

Chapter 2

"Seth is a bad man," I told Mama when she returned from the fabric store. Then I told her what happened.

She'd set about to fix dinner from what she'd bought at the A&P, eggs and bacon on toast and a can of peas. I wondered if she'd talked to the management at the grocery store about a job. Probably not, I decided. I didn't bring it up.

She'd become a penny pincher, which made me worry that life as we knew it would end as soon as our money ran out. Yet she seemed in no hurry to earn.

"You should have kept away from Seth, like I said. It was your responsibility to keep your dog out from under foot."

"He wasn't hurting anyone."

"He's a dog. They try to get away with whatever they can. You know that. I'm sure Seth didn't kick him all that hard."

"How would you know? You weren't here. You didn't see."

I thought she might send me to my room without dinner or punish me in some other way for standing up to her, yet she didn't.

By then Fritz had been gone for at least two hours. That being a long time for a boy my age, I feared the worst. "What if he doesn't come back?"

"I'm sorry," Mama said, "but perhaps that's for the best."

"He'll starve!"

"You know that's not true. He's a stray, so he knows how to take care of himself. It cost us money to feed him, and if I'm going to buy that automobile from Olin Turner, we'll need all the funds we can get.

The payout from your father's life insurance will only go so far."

Maybe she wasn't any more upset with me for arguing with her because Fritz running away pleased her so much. One less mouth to feed.

Daddy had been the one to allow me to keep the dog. She'd never liked Fritz. On really cold winter nights, I'd wanted him to sleep in my room so he wouldn't freeze to death. Daddy had gone to bat for me with Mama over that. My dog had gone everywhere with me back when Daddy had a say in things. Fritz knew the neighborhood, the creek, and the woods as well or better than I did. Why, once, he'd been wounded on the shoulder defending me against feral dogs. I would do anything for him.

Since Daddy died, my dog had not slept in the house.

~ ~ ~

The next morning, Mama and I sat in the kitchen eating larded bread for breakfast.

"If you can't find work, will we have to give up the house?" I asked. "Will we have to live on the street?"

Mama had become impatient with me because I'd been worrying aloud lately, something she didn't like. "No, Martin, that won't happen."

With the Crash, followed by Daddy's death, I felt like life had been broken.

Of course parents must say and do things for their children that give the impression that all's right with the world. But I had begun to think for myself, no matter what Mama might have said. I believed she turned a blind eye to the possible dangers ahead, while I did not. I'd seen the spreading hobo camp on the western side of the capital grounds downtown and how many down and out people wandered the streets. I knew something about the bank foreclosures and the growing crime in the city.

What worried me most about being on the street didn't have to do with the weather or loss of the comforts of home. I happily slept outdoors in the woods. The streets were an altogether different thing. The thought of Mama and me sleeping out in the open, surrounded by other desperate, bad people, like Seth, some willing to commit crimes to find food and shelter—that terrified me.

I'd had friends in school that lost their homes and had to move away. One, named Chuck, came back to class to say hello.

"We had to beg my uncle in Clarksville to take us in," he said. "That's fifteen people living in a small, two-room house. We don't have much and sometimes have to go hungry. We might soon be on the street."

Mama and I had no family we could beg for help. Daddy's parents had died. He'd been an only child. What family Mama still had, mostly Washington State salmon fishermen who lived much of the year on boats in Puget Sound, would have a hard time finding a place for us.

Remembering that Chuck had been surprised his family could lose everything so quickly, I told Mama, "Lots of people thought it couldn't happen to them."

"Just stop it," she said.

"No, I want to know what's going to happen."

"You're being ridiculous."

"Are you talking like that so I won't be scared or are you ignoring the dangers, hoping they'll go away?"

She gazed out the kitchen window. "Oh, Martin…"

"You have some ideas about the future. Tell me!"

"I can't know exactly what will happen. Those tornados in March, for instance, I had no notion that was coming." She smiled innocently.

"You're looking for excuses," I said. "Beyond 'acts of God,' you know some things I don't. I don't need an exact prediction. Tell me what you do know."

"I know that no bank will foreclose on us."

"Tell me about *that*."

Shaking her head, she took a deep breath, let out a grumpy huff, and said in a hurry, "Your grandparents paid off the mortgage, and when they passed away, your father inherited the house. Now that he's gone, it's ours. We have to pay for our needs, maintenance and repairs on the house, and taxes. With your Daddy's life insurance money, we have something to help us get along for now, but there will come a time I'll need a job. You being as self sufficient as possible will help, especially once I find a job and have to work days."

I couldn't understand all of what she said without more questions. At least I'd found out that we wouldn't lose the house soon.

I could tell she'd grown angry and I didn't want to make that worse. Trying to think of what to ask, I kept quiet too long. She got up from the table and left the room.

I decided that whatever she didn't want to say had her upset, not me. Possibly it had to do with finding work, something that would be hard for her since she'd never had a job before. Or maybe she got upset when I said things that made her think about how her life had changed with Daddy's death.

~ ~ ~

Fritz didn't return that night or the next day. I worried myself sick, thinking he'd been badly harmed and might be dying somewhere in the woods.

In the early evening of the second day, I said, "Tomorrow, I'm going to look for Fritz."

"No, you're not," Mama said, her voice holding a warning.

I got the feeling she enjoyed saying no to me. For all her talk about me being self-sufficient, she didn't truly want me to make decisions for myself. Her getting a job wouldn't come soon enough. She couldn't forbid things she didn't know about.

"Now, wipe Oklahoma off the table in preparation for dinner." She meant what blew on the wind from the Dust Bowl and settled on everything. We'd got in the habit of dusting off the table before each meal.

"What if Fritz thinks I wanted that man to kick him?" I asked.

"Dogs don't hold grudges," she said.

Glad to be rid of Fritz, she'd dismissed the whole thing. I'd grown so angry, I could just spit.

No matter what she thought, I had to find my dog.

Chapter 3

I worried through the night, getting little sleep. Mama fiddled about the house all morning, which delayed the start of my search for Fritz.

I hadn't seen much of the world since Daddy died and I sorely missed going on the sort of adventures I'd had with him. After school had let out for the summer, Mama kept me home as much as possible to be what she called, "My little helper." That kept me from spending much time with my friends, the Cordell children, Sammie and Buddy.

Evenings with Mama were the worst. She read to pass the time, but not like Daddy had done. He had read aloud to me until I learned how to read. "How 'bout I read to you," I asked her.

"My mind wanders if others read to me. I can't concentrate."

"Yeah, well you're boring when you read. If we had a radio…"

Daddy had allowed me to listen to the radio at the Cordell's house. Mondays through Thursdays, I'd come home from school, then run the half mile to their house for the next installment of Buck Rogers, which WLAC radio broadcast in the afternoon. Buddy tried to tell me what happened in the episodes I missed. That wasn't the same at all.

"Now is not the time for such an expense." Mama said. "If you're bored, perhaps you should read."

"I've read so much lately, I'll need glasses soon."

On Thursday evenings, she played bridge with some of the neighborhood women. I asked if she would teach me how to play.

"Bridge is for adults," she said.

My mother wasn't my friend, I decided. She wasn't any good at it.

Though I didn't like school, I found myself looking forward to returning to the classroom at the end of what promised to be a long, dull summer.

"Olin needs his automobile next week for one last trip with his grandchildren to the Glendale Zoo," she told me. "But once I buy it from him, I can start my search for a job in earnest."

Good luck, I thought, considering how many unemployed competed for work. That's when I realized she should have started looking much earlier.

"You understand that while I'm gone to work most of each day," she continued, "you'll have to take care of yourself. I won't be available. If you were any younger, I'd have to hire a minder to watch after you."

I'd be freed as soon as she got a job. Ha! That seemed unlikely. I decided she'd said that so easily because finding a job was a pipe dream— she had no plan to leave me on my own.

That afternoon, she went next door to help old Mrs. Fitzpatrick with her canning, and I saw my chance. I slipped out of the house to start my search for Fritz. Crossing the street—truly just a dirt road—I passed through the woods to get to Browns Creek, then followed the stream north through the woods along the edges of fields where cows grazed.

~ ~ ~

Walking along beside the flowing water, I couldn't help thinking about Daddy. Although the stream passed through property belonging to many different people, I'd always pretended the creek secretly belonged to us, Daddy and me. I ached to be with him again, and I suppose searching for Fritz along that happy brook was, in some ways, my search for him as well. At times, I could hear his happy chuckle in the sounds the water made.

Each weekday, he had walked about a half mile to his work at a pharmacy across Lealand Lane from Lipscomb College. A pharmacist, he had to be careful and serious in his work. Yet around me, he'd often been as playful as any child I'd known.

On the weekends, Daddy spent much of his time with me. He

took me to the pool hall and taught me how to play, something Mama wouldn't allow now that he'd passed away.

Daddy shared with me his interests and hobbies, like frog gigging, building and flying balsa wood airplanes, and amateur archaeology. With the archeology, he started calling our outings "expeditions."

We explored Browns Creek together and went gigging at night. Once he'd passed away, Mama took away the gigging forks, saying, "I don't know what your father was thinking, letting you handle something so sharp and dirty."

Daddy and I had carbide lamps—some call them miner's lamps—for spelunking in local, wild caves. Many caves had one or two rooms big enough to explore. Some had miles of passage. In one cave, we found a fossilized hip bone and femur that a Vanderbilt professor said belonged to an extinct type of giant sloth.

Because our friends, the Cordells, had an automobile, sometimes we asked them to go spelunking with us, especially when we had to travel a long way to the cave. For years, the mother of the Cordell family, Marjorie, had been my babysitter. She didn't care about caves, but the father, Hank, and the children, Samantha, thirteen years old, and Buddy, eleven, got excited about spelunking. Buddy's real name was Harold. Samantha we called Sammie. They had always been a part of my life. Their grandparents had been good friends with my Grandparents. I'd always known the Cordell's like family, even though they were not.

Gertie, their Saint Bernard dog, would occasionally run away from home and find her way to my house for a visit. When we took in Fritz, she'd come more often.

Daddy also led expeditions to uncover Indian relics and American Civil War artifacts. Sometimes the Cordells joined us for those outings.

The Battle of Nashville, a siege during the Civil War, had occurred in and around what became our neighborhood of Oak Hill. A couple miles away, at Shy's Hill, we found musket shot, and mini balls. At other battlefields, along with the shot, we also uncovered cannon ball shards and grapeshot.

Farther back in time, before the city of Nashville existed, salt springs had always drawn game to the area. Rather than living there, the Indians used the land as sacred hunting and burial grounds. That had been their tradition for thousands of years until the white man came and took it all away from them in the 1700s.

Construction crews digging basements for new houses often disturbed Indian burial sites. Daddy and I would look in on their excavations after hours. We could reach several construction sites within a half-hour's walk from home. The burials consisted of rough stone boxes under several feet of earth or sometimes within a mound. Since their stone sides didn't fit together tightly, those boxes got filled up over time with the same sort of packed soil and roots found in the surrounding earth. The burials were old enough that only the skeleton remained, embedded in all that tight soil, along with things needed in the afterlife. Anything not stone, bone, shell, or pottery always rotted away.

Daddy got permission from farmers for us to look for arrowheads in their freshly-turned fields. That worked especially well right after a rain. We got awful muddy while discovering many different shapes and sizes of stone points.

"Each type can be traced to a particular time period," Daddy told me. "The Clovis stone points are the most ancient, up to twelve thousand years old. They would have tipped the spears launched with atlatls at a time before the Indians of the region used bow and arrow. Their use of this area runs far back into prehistoric time."

I loved all the history.

"What does an atlatl look like?" I asked.

"It's like a long handle with a slight crook and a notch at the end to hold a spear shaft."

"I want to find a book at the library with a picture of an atlatl," I told Daddy.

"Tell you what," he said. "How 'bout we make one and some spears to throw. We have enough stone points that we could spare a few."

He got a book from the library that had not only pictures, but also instructions on how to make an atlatl. We spent several weekends fiddling with the project and finally made a six-foot thrower and ten spears almost the same length, with replaceable fore-shafts. Daddy made a slightly smaller thrower—maybe five feet long—for me.

Once Mama found out what we were doing, she said, "You're not going to launch those spears with that thing."

Daddy seemed to notice the warning that went with her words. "Of course not," he said. "We're just looking into history to see what we can see."

I figured we wouldn't be trying out the atlatl until she left to run an errand or something.

When I brought up the subject, Daddy said, "We need more space than we have here at home. The Cordells have a bigger back yard. I wonder if they might like to take part in our practice and learn about the atlatls. Then your mother won't have to know about what we're doing." He gave me a sly smile.

Hank showed excitement for the idea. He got an archery target that he attached to a bale of hay in his back yard. Sammie and Buddy also joined in.

"I figure your Sally doesn't want you doing this," Hank said to Daddy.

"What Sal doesn't know won't hurt her. And, yes, I thought we'd practice here so she wouldn't get all upset and spoil our fun."

"I don't mind being used," Hank said with big smile. "Not by you, anyway."

Daddy clapped him on the back. "I should have told you that first. Sorry. Thanks for letting us use your back yard."

Starting out, we were all pretty bad. We broke one stone point, cracked a spear shaft and Sammie nearly impaled poor Gertie. Still, we got better. Surprised us all to see that Buddy had the best success hitting what he aimed at.

"You are so good at this," I told him. "Can you show us how to throw them better?"

"Hey," Sammie said. "I almost hit the target. "Soon I'll be hitting the bull's eye every time."

"That's okay, Sammie," Hank said. "Your brother is undeniably better at this than any of us."

Sammie stuck her tongue out at Buddy.

Hank gave her a stern look, said, "Go ahead, son, tell us what you know."

"I can try," Buddy said, "but it's like I already knew how, I just had to remember."

He showed us how he stood and held the atlatl when he threw a spear. We all got better, except for Sammie, who seemed to intentionally ignore her brother's advice.

We moved the target from fifty feet away to seventy. With it that far away, none of us could even hit the hay bale, except for Buddy.

At the end of the day, Daddy and I left the atlatls and spears at the Cordell's house.

Yes, I missed him like nobody's business. Occasionally, I'd get out the airplane dope we'd used in making model airplanes and open the jar to let the smell out. No other odor could so powerfully bring back my memories of being with Daddy. The day I discovered how it aided those recollections, I smelled the stuff for too long and keeled over in my bedroom. A good thing Mama didn't know about that. Discovering the spot on the floor where I'd dropped the dope and the goop had spilled, she gave me a spanking. Daddy had spanked me on rare occasions for being a brat. She didn't put enough force into her smacks to make them painful. All the same, I pretended he was spanking me and I cried out with each smack so she wouldn't know the difference.

～ ～ ～

Careful to look out for snakes and snapping turtles, I made my way under the old stone bridge at Caldwell Lane, then entered the stretch of woods that surrounded the antebellum mansion belonging to the McClanahan family. A section of that forested land not far to the south separated our neighborhood from the train yard.

I thought Fritz might have gone to the Cordell's house. He liked Gertie. The path that led to their house wasn't far past the mansion's old spring house, which stood on the west side of the woods along the creek. I often stopped at the McClnahan spring house when nearby. Fritz might do the same, I thought. The temperature of the air inside remained much the same year-round: cool in summer, fairly warm in winter. A small stream flowed from beneath a shelf of rock on the northern side of the entrance, danced over the slippery rocks, and fell into the creek in a small cascade. No doubt the McClanahan family had used the spring house to keep perishable food cool long before ice boxes and refrigerators came along.

The entrance had been finished out with stone, forming an arched doorway with a keystone in the center at the top. Though the room inside went about twelve feet back into the hillside, the few stalactites hanging from the ceiling and the breakdown at the back suggested that, at one time, the opening in the hillside had been part of a larger cave complex.

The spring flowed from beneath the breakdown at the back of the room, traveled through a channel hand-cut into the rock floor, and passed into a hole in the wall to the right of the entrance. From there, the water traveled unseen until it found its way out from under the shelf of rock outside.

The gravel in the creek bed and along the banks near the spring house held countless flint flakes.

"That shows the Indians once came here to make stone tools," Daddy had said. "The spring's cave room itself might have also been important to them." Of course that would have been long before the place became a spring house.

A week earlier, I had remembered his words, and dug into the dirt floor to see what I could find. More flint chips, some large enough to make into stone points, and a few pottery shards. One of the larger chips I had uncovered looked like a fish and was an unusual, greenish color. I'd never seen green flint before. More remarkable still, someone had scratched a rectangle into the stone. Not a sloppy one, but a rectangle with proper ninety-degree corners—very well done. Some Indian had done that, I figured.

At the time, I got the notion that if I drew on the chip and put it back in the ground, that might be a way to communicate with that Indian from long ago. With the pocketknife Daddy gave me (one Mama knew nothing about), I had scratched a dot close to one of the rectangle's corners, then reburied the stone as close as possible to where I'd found it.

Now, remembering all that, I got excited to see if the fish-shaped piece of green flint had changed any. I dug into the floor in the spot I remembered burying it and came upon the unusual stone right away. The drawings on it *did* look different. Short lines stretched outward from the dot, making it a tiny star. I didn't know what we were saying to each other, and yet, I was persuaded that I'd communicated with a long-dead Indian, one that hunted there hundreds or maybe even thousands of years before the city of Nashville came about.

Excited, I added another rectangle to the stone, not as perfect. The dot/star now sat within a square formed where the corners of the rectangles overlapped. I reburied the flint, packed and smoothed the floor to hide my digging, and left the spring house, stepping into warm, late afternoon light.

If I wanted to avoid trouble with Mama, I knew I should go home. Instead, I continued on toward the Cordell's house.

They had a telephone. Mama didn't. And if I told them she'd sent me to ask if I could spend the night because she had to be away, I reckoned they wouldn't question that. They would simply say yes.

Chapter 4

I'd never gotten lost before. If I'd ever been somewhere even once, I could find my way back there easily enough. At least that had been true until that evening. And here I passed through the woods I considered *mine*, near *my* creek.

I got the feeling that someone watched me and I glanced around several times. Seth came to mind, but I had no way of knowing if he had stuck around after kicking Fritz. Thinking I saw a shadowy figure duck behind a tree, I hurried up my pace.

As dusk fell, I knew I'd walked too far, well past the cut through the trees that led to the Cordell's house. I saw nothing that felt like a familiar place. Still, I kept going as dusk turned to night, with a full moon above the trees to my right.

Thinking about being followed, I decided I should get to the creek and cross to the other side. Once I reached the creek bank, I tied my shoelaces together and hung my shoes around my neck. In the dim light, hopping across on the rocks caught in the stream, I couldn't help pausing in the middle to see the lightning bugs reflected in the rippling water. I turned one way, then back the other before leaving the creek bed and climbing up the bank. That's how I remembered what I did, anyway. Yet looking back down, I noticed the water didn't flow in the direction I expected.

The feeling of being lost took hold of me and I stood looking about, wondering if I'd somehow gotten turned around. If that were true, I decided, continuing on, I would see landmarks I'd passed. That didn't happen.

Surely, I just went farther down the creek than I'd ever been before. Maybe I'd accidentally found my way to a feeder stream or a branch off the main creek, and that explained the direction the water moved.

And again, I had the feeling of being watched.

I dismissed the urge to turn and go back the other way. *Don't let ridiculous fears push you,* I told myself. *Seth is probably in Memphis by now, fast as he was walking. Keep your eyes and ears open.*

The creek widened out into a large pond or morass, cane breaks and dead trees along the edges. In a little cove, I discovered a thin dirt road that followed the edge of the water. If not for the moonlight angling down through the trees, I might not have noticed the little houses on the other side of the road since they had no lights on. They seemed to be hiding in the thick vegetation at the edge of the woods.

From a distance they appeared to be regular-sized houses with gaily painted woodwork and fancy things like bay windows, dormers, and balconies. Getting closer, I saw that in truth each house stood about ten feet high, the size of a small work shed or shack. Too small to be useful to regular people, all of the fancy parts were simply decoration.

I thought the place empty or possibly abandoned, and had to wonder who lived or stayed there and when. Could the shacks be the off-season home of small circus or carnival performers? They had a look that reminded me of the houses Daddy had once shown me in a book about Rugby, Tennessee, a farming community on the Cumberland plateau established in the late 1800s for the "second sons" of British nobility. The town had thrived for a time, then failed. Daddy had called the style of houses "Victorian." Although the community failed, much of the town remained and some people lived there still. Daddy had promised to take us to see Rugby one day.

From the forest to my left, I heard rustling leaves and snapping twigs, as if someone walked slowly or crept along nearby. I felt the need to hide, and approached the nearest shack. When I tried the door, it swung open with a high-pitched squeal. Cringing over the idea that I'd given myself away, I slipped into the darkness within. A heavy smell of mildew hit me. I felt around, found a chair and table, even if I could scarcely see them. In one corner, I stepped on something soft. Down on my knees, I reluctantly felt that softness. A quilt maybe on an old fashion straw mattress.

A window in the back wall broke, the sound of shattering and falling glass sending my head spinning to see what had happened. In the near complete dark, I saw very little.

A moaning came from the forest behind the shack. Shaking, I cowered down on the floor. I lifted the quilt to drape over me, trying to make myself as small as possible. A soft, rapid thumping sound caught my ear and I realized that the heel of my right foot bounced up and down. Trying to quiet that shaking, I pressed my feet and hands firmly against what felt like a packed-dirt floor.

The moaning, a deep pained sound, continued and became louder, moving to one side of the shack, and the other. Looking through folds in the quilt, I discovered I'd left the door open. I watched from the darkness, and saw a shadowy form lean in. Unable to see anything familiar or friendly about the silhouette, I readied myself to bolt past through the door and into the deepening darkness outside.

Barking in the distance.

The shadow pulled back from the opening and disappeared. The barking grew louder and I heard a thrashing sound, like someone's heedless running through the underbrush. I recognized Gertie's deep canine voice.

She let out a sharp cry of pain. The thrashing sounds didn't let up, though, and her growling grew louder. She fought with something or someone who didn't make a peep. More than anything, that made me think she chased a human being. Seth? The sounds of the fight moved through the forest heading away from me in a northwesterly direction.

I huddled in the darkness until the sounds faded away, then went to the last shack in the row and went inside. Less of the odor of mildew there. Similar stuff inside, including the straw mattress. No quilt. That's when I realized I still had the one from the other shack draped over my head and shoulders. I lay down on the mattress, tried to quiet my shivering limbs, and take slow, deep breaths. About the time

I'd gained some calm, I heard something approaching outside and my quaking began again.

I had pushed the door to, but the latch didn't catch. If Gertie didn't come back, I was done for, I decided.

I sat up and felt around for something to use as a weapon, found nothing. Instead, I lay flat on the mattress and arranged the quilt to cover all of me. What else could I do?

A snuffling sound along the bottom edge of the door seemed to come from a snout attached to a big pair of lungs—Gertie had returned after chasing away the danger.

I sat up again and nudged the door with a foot. She pushed it open from outside and stood looking in, maybe uncertain. As she moved her head this way and that, the blue-green gleam deep in her eyes flickered.

"Come here, girl," I said.

She came and sat beside me, turned and licked fully half my head with that big tongue of hers.

"Good dog," I said, wiping slobber from my cheek and forehead. I gave her a proper petting of gratitude behind the ears and around her neck. She lay down on the mattress and put her head in my lap, drool from her hanging upper lips getting all over me. Glad to have her there, I didn't care.

Feeling confident that she would hear and alert me if anyone were coming, at some point I lay back down and slid off to sleep.

Chapter 5

By the time I awoke, Gertie had gone.

I lay where I'd slept for a little while longer, thinking about the dream I'd had in the night. In it, I seemed to have stumbled upon a dump site in the forest. Seth would have been pleased. This big machine, like a large ball with yellow lights on its surface, sat in the middle of the dump. Above the ball floated a halo like you might see in a picture of a saint. Probably because of my love of Buck Rogers, I got the idea the machine could think.

A crazy dream!

The door, open a crack, allowed a bright beam of light to crawl across the floor, the mattress, and part way up the far wall. In that light, I could see what looked like dried blood on the mattress where I had laid my head. I felt my face, ears, and scalp, looking for a wound and didn't find one. On the table, I saw broken lures and some weights. A tangle of fishing line rested in the seat of a chair. A cane pole leaned into one corner, a crack running partway along its length.

The door to the shack had been forced open at some point in the past, the wood of the frame around the bolt catch broken. More dried blood on the wood. Whatever violence put the blood there happened before I showed up.

Listening at the door, I decided I was alone.

Filled with the spirit of adventure, I chose not to worry too much about the dangers. I know now that I should have been more afraid.

Outside, the row of houses looked stranger still by daylight, with their bright, clashing colors and sod roofs that held growing plants.

What I'd taken for balconies hung below the windows, looked like flower boxes full of dead weeds. A different fisherman's prayer had been painted above each doorway and a horseshoe nailed above that, I supposed for good luck.

A large fire pit, dug into the earth about fifteen feet in front of the shacks, had sections of log, like seats, arranged around it. Discarded bottles and empty food cans lay on the ground. A broken bottle had blood on its sharp edges. Behind the shacks, I discovered a garbage dump and a large pile of empty liquor bottles. A rope with a hangman's noose hung from a tree limb above the dump. The lower part of the noose had been stained with blood.

The smell of the dump, like rotting meat, drove me away.

A hobo camp? I knew that folks were up in arms about "vagrants," and that they used that word against hoboes, even the hard-working ones. Had an angry mob made mischief there to make an example of what happened to squatters?

Or had the place simply been a fishing camp and drinking spot where friends gathered? Had there been a prohibition raid that drove them away and explained all the broken stuff and the blood?

I looked in all the shacks, and found no answers.

I walked along the edge of the pond until it became a creek again, then picked my way southward on the bank through thick undergrowth. That grew too difficult, so I tied my shoes together again, hung them around my neck, and used the creek as my trail. Walking upstream helped me to see much of what came my way; mostly leaves, sticks, minnows, and crawfish—nothing to be afraid of.

With the sounds of birds, insects, the wind in the leaves, and the slosh of my walking, I feared I'd miss hearing possible threats ahead, and I still worried about being followed. Thinking about the blood at the fishing camp, I wondered if Seth and his trench knife had been mixed up in it somehow. At the same time, considering the bloody noose, the blood appearing in a few places at the camp, as well as on the sharp edges of a broken bottle, I had the feeling that the "mischief" had been the work of more than one man.

I paused here and there to listen. While stopped, I heard the murmur of voices in the forest toward the southeast. I wished Fritz were with me, and not just because he made a good companion. Watching his head and ears would have told me exactly what direction the voices came from. Seeing the way he moved and how he held his body, would have let me know if the owners of the voices moved toward me, and whether or not they meant me harm. I felt a bit blind without him.

I decided to circle around to the right of the voices and see if I could find the speakers without being seen. I'd already gotten close enough to tell that most of the voices belonged to men. One had a peculiar accent. That speaker was doing what Daddy had called pontificating, something he didn't like. "No one should be so self-satisfied that they believe they know everything," Daddy had said. "Even if you haven't thought of something, that doesn't mean it's not worth considering." Sometimes the things he said baffled me for a time, and only later made sense.

From a point slightly to the west, I got a view through the tangle of vines and undergrowth. I saw more little shacks arranged along a thin dirt road. They weren't fancied up like the ones where I'd spent the night. Made from various castoffs—maybe from construction, farming, and what folks left out for garbage collectors—the shacks were held together with wire, heavy cord, and rope. Some had tin roofs, some had shakes and one had clapboard fastened horizontally across its top at an angle meant to shed water. The windows held greased paper instead of glass.

Keeping its trunk between me and the little community, I climbed a hackberry tree to get a better view. I stood on a limb about eight inches across and looked through gaps in the leaves. Trying to find signs of Fritz and finding none, I wanted to push the leaves that hid me aside to widen my view. I knew better than to do that. Instead, I quietly climbed higher and settled into a crotch of four limbs. A flat spot where the branches came together gave me a space so small I could stand there with only one foot. The surrounding limbs and creeping vines hid me fairly well.

Leaning out enough to get a look, I saw that another dirt road crossed the first one at the center of the community. An island in the middle of the intersection had two men seated in wicker chairs. One wore an old ragged black suit, including a maroon waistcoat, what might have once been nice shoes, and a black bowler hat with a dent in the crown. The other wore a dirty, pale-gray suit of clothes and an off-white fedora. Others, at least six men and two women, stood in the road facing them, a wheelbarrow loaded with cans of food between them.

I strained to hear what they said and could make out no more than one or two words before their conversation seemed to get heated. With the louder voices, I heard everything.

"No!" the man in the bowler said. "before you stow those tins away, I'll have my pick."

At the flicks, Daddy and I had seen a talkie that starred an English actor that sounded something like that.

"What folks here don't know won't hurt them," the man in gray clothing said.

"Some have seen this batch, Rex," said one of the women. "They trust you because they believe you are honest with them."

The man in gray huffed. "They trust him because of what he gives them."

"Yeah, well," the woman said, "if they find out on their own that you skim off the best for yourself, they won't trust you anymore."

"You think he doesn't know that?" the man in gray said.

"Just tell them you do it," yet another man said. "They want what you're offering enough to allow it."

The Englishman had been quiet, rubbing his forehead as if lost in thought. "No, Harry is right. The big lies, the ridiculous ones, work best, but if poking holes in the small ones is easy, that could expose the larger falsehoods to scrutiny."

The Englishman had to be Rex. I assumed the woman went by the name, Harry—from Harriet, maybe? I didn't understand the meaning of what they said.

"Save me a can of those peaches," Rex demanded. He stood, turned to the man in the gray clothing, and said something too quiet for me to hear. They walked off together, circling around a shack and entering it on the far side.

Those in the road went their separate ways, two of the men walking toward my tree.

I crouched down, hugging one limb and making myself as small as possible.

One of the men, dressed in overalls, had his head shaved except for the top. A few locks of long hair from his crown hung down over one eye.

The other, a man with a head of oiled black hair, wore a worn-out red and green plaid shirt and pants a few sizes too large. They stayed up thanks to a length of rope cinched around the waist.

"I wish he wouldn't talk out in the open like that." Overalls said. "How does he know someone isn't listening?" He glanced around, even up at the trees, and I could have sworn his eyes came to rest on me for an instant. I pulled back, crouching on one foot in the small space.

"They're all out making their scavenging rounds," Baggy Pants said.

"What about Seth?"

Seth? They knew Seth?

Again, Overalls glanced around at the surrounding forest, this time with a fearful look on his face.

So, Seth scared them too.

"We keep losing some of our people to the police," Overalls said, "so something about his system isn't working."

"Seth didn't get picked up by the police," Baggy Pants said. "Not that I know of."

"I'm not talking about Seth. Seth left for his own reasons."

"We're not losing enough of our people to matter. And we all know how far Rex will go to punish those who step out of line. I can't see any one of us leading the police here. What Rex did at the fishing camp made for a powerful example. Smart!"

From that, I took it that Rex and his people had been behind whatever happened at the fishing camp. Thinking they used violence to get their way, I got a terrible, sinking feeling about what might happen if they found me. These were the sorts of desperate people I worried about meeting up with if Mama and I lost the house and had to sleep out on the streets.

"You call that smart?" Overalls said, "It drew attention in our direction."

"Nobody cares 'cause he was just a darkie."

I figured Baggy Pants meant they'd made an example of a black man at the fishing camp.

"Rex pays the police to look the other way," he said.

"Yeah, and that's all the protection we have."

"We've got plenty willing to do whatever it takes."

"You know," Overalls said, "when you asked me to come here with you, I didn't want to."

"Yeah," Baggy Pants said, "until Mr. Hoover sent troops to shoot at us, his thanks to us for winning the war."

Does he mean the president? Did President Hoover send soldiers to shoot at Americans?

"The United States didn't win the Great War alone. Rex and them talk like that to make us think something was taken from us. When we had just arrived here, do you remember him saying that blacks took all the best jobs while we were away fighting the Hun? He said they took them and kept them. Here we are, back in the U.S. for over ten years and he has the gall to say such a thing, like we couldn't know the truth. I knew then he was playing us. Later he added the lie about blacks sleeping with our wives and daughters. Most of us knew those things didn't happen, yet no one challenged him. I don't know how he does it, keeping all his lies straight."

"You didn't challenge him either."

"No, not with all the veterans backing him up, soldiers he's riled up with all his lies."

"They're already angry over what was taken from them. He's just harnessing that anger and putting it to good purpose. So what if he lies a little?"

"My anger doesn't run so deep that it keeps me from using my brain. Demonstrating in Washington turned out to be a big mistake. The government was never going to give in. And yeah, as soon as they started firing on us, I wanted out. I'd seen enough of men with guns. I followed you here since I had nothing else. I joined up with Rex because I got tired of being hungry all the time."

"Well, you should be *damned* angry over what the government has done, and what they allowed to happen to our lives while using us for their war. For someone with no home or job, you're doing all right, thanks to Rex. We are his muscle, his bully boys. You are lucky to play a part. When we get to the turn…"

"I know what he's all about now, and I know my part," Overalls said. "Yeah, we've had it good, but Rex's racket will all spill out eventually and I hope we aren't here to suffer along with the rest of them. At times I just want to cut and run. Truth is, if you weren't my cousin…. Well, let's say you're the only thing keeping me here."

"Seriously, you would leave and give up the position you'll gain once we find the Will'ven't Bin and get to the *turn?*"

The what?

"Yeah," Overalls said sounding disgusted, "like those ain't just more of his lies."

"I believe in him," Baggy Pants said. "He has the same gripes we have. That's why we believe in him. Doesn't matter if he lies. The rest of us figure if he chooses to do that, he must have a good reason."

"You know he's a remittance man?" Overalls said.

"What does that mean?"

"I learned that from Harry. Means his family in England sends him money to stay away. That's how he has the funds to pay off the police. He is indeed from a British noble family. Being a drunkard and a gambler with a lot of debt, they found him to be an embarrassment."

I wondered if Rex had come from Rugby.

"Men change," Baggy pants said.

"Yeah, usually for the worse, not the better. If he's willing to tell us he's using the others and they'll get nothing in the end, who's to say he won't do that to his inner circle also?"

"You should cut and run now or stop talking that way," Baggy Pants said. "I won't tell Rex what you said. We're family, after all. I'm hoping you'll come back to our way of thinking. You owe him better than that, Lawrence, and you know it."

"Do I, Ned?"

Ned turned on his heels and walked away from Lawrence.

Although I could not follow all of their conversation, I did understand that these people were up to no good, and willing to use bribery and violence to get their way.

And the *turn*? What could that be?

They seemed like gangsters, but didn't look like the ones at the flicks.

I had to get away from there, quick as possible.

~ ~ ~

I hadn't gotten far from Rex's community when I heard the voice.

"Boy...."

Thinking it came from one of Rex's muscle, I spun around to face the underbrush behind me.

Seth stood and moved toward me. I backed up, my heart pounding in my chest. His left shirt sleeve had a long tear and a blood stain. I wondered if Gertie had done that the night before. If she thought him dangerous, I needed to get away from him. I couldn't decide whether or not I'd have a chance if I ran.

"Your mother out looking for you, came upon me walking your road," he said.

The moment I planted my feet and leaned forward to run, Seth grabbed my shirt collar. I struggled uselessly in his powerful grip, popping loose my shirt's top two buttons.

"I'm not here to fetch you home to her," he said, turning me around. "She said you'd run away to look for your dog. I'd wager the dog ran off after what I done to him. That was a cruel thing. I'm sorry."

I relaxed some. He'd looked at me squarely, allowing me to see his milky gaze. His voice still had a hoarseness.

"That's right," he said, "get a good look. Mustard gas done this to me in the Great War. To my skin too. The doctors said I didn't get enough to harm me. Even so, the sores and blindness keep growing. If my crooked face is scary, it's 'cause the mustard gas took away what control I had on the right side."

Maybe I'd misjudged him. I didn't know if he'd been the one to show up at the fishing camp in the night, making noises and knocking about. The wound on his arm might have happened any number of ways. I'd grown too afraid of him to ask questions he might take as accusations. He had been one of Rex's men, yet now they seemed to fear him too.

"I can't see much beyond about ten feet" he said. "I need your help to find the Will'ven't Bin."

Chapter 6

Seeing as Seth needed my help, I lost some of my fear of him. I had a lot of questions about the "Will'ven't Bin," especially since I'd also heard Ned mention it along with something he referred to as "the Turn." Seth could not answer all my questions, but he said that once we found the Will'ven't Bin my curiosity would be satisfied.

After promising to meet him at the McClanahan spring house later that afternoon, I'd found Brown's Creek again and followed the water downstream.

When I arrived at the Cordell's place, Gertie bounded across the lawn toward me and might have knocked me down if I hadn't shouted, "No!" She came to a sudden halt, her big paws cutting divots out of the lawn. I gave her another petting of gratitude. Nuzzling me for more, she got drool all over my hands. I started to wipe them on my pants.

Sammie and Buddy must have heard us and come out of the house.

"Wipe it on the grass," Sammie said. She had had her hair cut short for the hot weather, something she'd been pushing her mother to do for some time. She looked cute.

"Oh, yeah, okay," I said, embarrassed. I didn't like to think she saw me as unclean.

Mr. Cordell at work at his veterinary office and Mrs. Cordell gone to help a pregnant friend, Sammie had babysitting duties, something Buddy didn't like.

He took me into his room where he showed off our latest electrical tower, now finished. I'd left him the task of putting the crossarm on once the Duco® Cement had dried on the rest of the model. Made of toothpicks and close to two feet tall, the thing looked like a man from another planet or a robot from Buck Rogers. Buddy's and Sammie's uncle, Bruce Cordell, who worked for the Tennessee Valley Authority, gave Buddy diagrams for actual electrical towers the TVA erected. I helped him build them. So far, we'd made eight different electrical towers, the first three from wooden match sticks with the heads cut off, the last five from flat toothpicks.

Seeing that we'd used matchsticks on the first one, Sammie had said, "You should build one with the match heads in place. When done, we could light it up."

"You want to get us in trouble," Buddy said.

"You're pretty good at that on your own," she said.

Not interested in our models, Sammie hovered in the door to Buddy's room, listening to us talk. I told about what had happened with Fritz, Seth, me looking for Fritz, the fishing camp, and Gertie coming to my defense. At some point during all that, Sammie came into the room.

"I wondered where she got that cut on her side," Buddy said.

I didn't remember seeing a cut. "Is she all right?"

"Yeah, I think so." Sammie said. "Daddy sewed up her wound, took about twenty stitches. She woke up from her ether nap about an hour ago."

As she'd chased someone away from the fishing camp in the night, I'd heard her squeal like she'd been hurt. Returning, she'd lain beside me in the shack. Possibly that's how blood got on the straw mattress.

When asked, Seth said he had not been to the fishing camp recently. If that were true, then someone else dangerous lurked in the woods along the creek.

I told them about Rex's community, and something, if not all, of the deal I struck with Seth. "He'll help me find Fritz, while I help him find something called the Will'ven't Bin."

"Are you just making up words?" Sammie asked, giving me a nasty sneer.

How to describe it. I itched to tell them about the dream, yet I didn't want to give the impression I didn't believe in the Will'ven't Bin. I also didn't want them to think of me as gullible enough to mistake my dream for reality.

"You mean a will-o'-the-wisp?" Buddy asked.

"No, not swamp gas. It's like a bin—a rubbish bin, maybe—but one where you put things that should never have *been*."

Both of them looked confused.

"Give me a pencil and a piece of paper and I'll try to explain," I said.

I sat at Buddy's desk and he gave me what I asked for. They leaned over to watch me write, "The Will'ven't Bin."

"That's a compound contraction," Sammie said. "My teacher says that's not proper grammar."

"Oh, I see," Buddy said, "you mean 'will have not been,' right?"

"Yeah, except for the spelling of 'been' as 'bin.' The way Seth described it, the Bin holds those man-made things that are a danger to mankind or the Earth—those things that should never have been."

"So, like a trash can for bad stuff?" Buddy asked.

"No, not small," I said. "More like a dump site."

I considered Buddy, two years younger than me, smart, if a bit goofy. Sammie, one year older than me, pretended to think me stupid. She probably didn't know I knew that to be an act. She liked causing trouble, tormenting Buddy and me endlessly with what she called practical jokes. Typical of her early "jokes" were things like putting apple butter in Buddy's hat. He'd made a mess in his hair putting that on.

Lately, she'd turned to science for ideas.

One day while their mother shopped for groceries and Sammie had babysitting duties, I had joined them for lunch. Before I got there, she put baking soda in a bottle of ketchup and put the top back on. The first to open the bottle, I got foamy, pink glop all over me. The sauce went everywhere. While she laughed, I'd helped her clean up the kitchen. I left to go home and change clothes so her mother wouldn't see me and learn of her mischief.

Not practical!

"I don't believe your story," Sammie said. "It's too weird. You're trying out your excuse on us before giving it to your mother."

"She was here last night looking for you," Buddy said.

"I'm not surprised."

"She was crying," he said.

Somehow that troubled me. I'd always seen Mama as too proud to allow people to see her like that. Had I caused her so much pain that she couldn't hide her feelings? With those thoughts, my throat clenched tight and I had to blink my watering eyes. Even though I'd recently thought she wasn't my friend, that didn't mean I had no feelings for her.

"She is terrible upset," Sammie told me with a smile. "She won't believe you either. You're in for a hiding."

I didn't fear that, and I wouldn't have to face it until I found Fritz and went home anyway.

"Please don't tell your Mama I was here," I asked.

"I won't," Buddy said.

Always defiant, Sammie said, "I'll consider it." Again, she smiled, and I knew she would not tell on me.

Buddy said, "Okay, so what kind of things go in the Will'ven't Bin?" His face took on a crooked, half smile, "Things, like my sister?"

"I'm not a 'thing.'"

"Hee-haw, you admitted to being nothing?" Buddy said. He'd landed a blow to his sister. His wide, toothy grin told me how seldom that happened.

Sammie had nothing to say, and her face showed no upset.

"Your sister is not that bad," I said. "She's smart and knows how to do things most people can't. She'll calm down eventually. She does smell really bad, though."

I saw her smile at my words. She had a good sense of humor. When Buddy turned to face her, she replaced the smile with a mean look, her left eye scrunched up tight and her mouth set crooked.

"I'm keeping an eye on you two," she said. "You're the ones cooking up trouble and you'll bring me in on it whether I want to be a part or not. I suppose I need to get used to being in trouble all the time."

I'll admit, something about that girl had always tugged at me. I feared I might grow feelings for her. She had gumption and lots of spirit. If she'd been a boy, I'm certain we would have been best friends.

"You are easily amazed by her," Buddy said, "No one cares about half the stuff she knows. Who will ever need to know where the constellations are in the sky or how long it takes for a tadpole to become a frog?"

"If you're a space traveler," I said, looking at Sammie and hoping for approval, "you have to know the constellations to get anywhere. And frogs—"

"I just want to know if we can get rid of Sammie by putting her in the Will'ven't Bin," Buddy said, stomping a foot.

"No," I told him, "the Will'ven't Bin isn't for holding people, but inventions. Seth says a lot of them are things invented for war. The Romans invented this stuff called Greek fire that burns even on water. No other weapon like it in its time. The stuff could be loaded into a grenade and tossed or it could be sprayed from some sort of cannon. History has stories of Greek Fire being used in naval battles. Others tried to figure out the formula and failed. Then, except in stories, it disappeared from history. No one knew how to make the stuff, still don't. Seth says the formula for Greek Fire is in the Will'ven't Bin, along with other destructive inventions. When I imagine the Will'ven't Bin, I picture the place having things like vehicles, appliances, and machines, file cabinets full of plans, diagrams, and formulas, lots of other stuff, big and small—centuries' worth—all thrown together in the forest."

"Okay," Sammie said impatiently, "enough of what you imagine. So we don't know where the Will'ven't Bin is. Do we know who decides what goes in this bin. Do we know how big it is?"

I immediately thought that the big machine sitting atop the junk in my dream was the one that decided. And even though it had been a dream, I couldn't shake the feeling that there had to be some truth to it.

"I don't know. I asked. Seth said he didn't know. He talks like people finding the place would only see a junk heap, since they wouldn't know what they were looking at."

"What else is in there?" she asked.

"Well, something not for war is a drug called Soma. They used it in the Orient and India centuries ago. You can't find Soma in the world today, Seth says, and no one knows how the drug got made or what plant the stuff might have come from."

"I don't believe any of this nonsense," Sammie said.

With her words, my doubts about Seth came to mind. His story had been hard enough to believe. After he'd said he had no idea where to find the Will'ven't Bin, I might have walked away, but he'd kept talking and I wasn't through listening. He offered to help me find Fritz and to protect me from Rex and his people while we did. Then he told me he wanted to find a time machine that had found its way into the Will'ven't Bin. Since I'd read *The Time Machine* by H.G. Wells, that's how I imagined it.

I wondered if I could use the thing to go back and be with Daddy again. Although the idea excited the hell out me, I hid that from Seth.

With the hope of seeing Daddy so strong, I couldn't help but believe in the Will'ven't Bin.

Chapter 7

I didn't mean for Sammie and Buddy to go with me to meet Seth. I'd set out from their house on my own, having said goodbye and telling them that I'd go home once the meeting ended so Mama wouldn't continue being upset.

I'd gotten to the creek when I heard crunching steps and turned around. Gertie stood right behind me, the Cordell children coming along after her. I realized I'd reached for my mouth to stifle my own startled cry. How had I gotten so distracted that I didn't hear them?

My thoughts elsewhere, I didn't hear the next thing Sammie said.

What was wrong with me? My odd experiences in the woods around the creek within the last day had shaken me. I didn't know what I could trust. My sense of direction had failed me. Walking along the creek I thought I knew well, I had run into dangers in places I didn't even know about. And now, my hearing and ability to stay alert had failed me.

I found myself sitting in the dirt, holding my head in my hands.

"Are you all right?" Buddy asked. He leaned down to look me in the eye.

Gertie licked my left ear, then his right one.

I lowered my hands and looked up.

Even Sammie had a worried look. "He's having a spell of some sort," she said. "Martin, you've been brave doing all this on your own. Now, we're with you. Come on."

I'd never imagined she'd speak to me that way. And the look on her face—like she truly cared. That got me moving.

She reached to grasp my right hand, Buddy took my left, and they pulled me to my feet.

"We're coming with you, no matter what you think." Buddy said.

I didn't have the willpower at that moment to argue with them.

~ ~ ~

From a distance, I saw Seth crouched in the doorway to the spring house. He stood as we approached and gave us a cold stare. His haversack rested on the ground at his feet.

Gertie growled.

Seth crouched again and reached for something in the haversack, his trench knife, I thought.

"You might want to keep Gertie back," I told Buddy.

He and Sammie gave me questioning looks.

Seth stood. I saw that he had a small piece of jerky in his hand. He tossed the dried meat and Gertie pounced, seeming to swallow the whole piece at once. That's when I saw the stitched-up cut on her side, mostly hidden beneath thick fur.

"I should have told you to come alone," Seth said.

"They're good friends, Sammie and Buddy. You can trust them to keep your secret."

"You told them, then?" Seth's face looked angry on the left side.

"Do you want my help?" I asked. Where had that gumption come from? Had I lost all my fear of the man?

"What about the dog?" he asked.

"I didn't tell her about it because she doesn't understand much language."

There, I'd made him chuckle, at least. Smiling crookedly, Seth took a step toward the doorway. "Let's go inside and talk," he said.

"You two stay here," I told my friends.

Seth backed into the darkness and I followed.

The floor had been disturbed where I'd buried the green, fish-shaped piece of flint. I remembered having smoothed out the soil before leaving last time. Had Seth known I'd buried the stone there? Had he dug the thing up? I could have asked, yet something told me to hide that from him.

"The fewer people who know about the Will'ven't Bin, the better," Seth said. "If you can't keep your mouth shut, I brought the wrong one in on this."

"I was upset," I said, "and it just spilled out."

"All the more reason I should look for another confederate."

"No," I said, reaching to grip his arm.

He pulled away.

"I didn't tell them what you're looking for in the Will'ven't Bin," I said.

If he'd known of my interest in what he looked for, he would not have wanted me along for that reason alone.

Seth seemed to relax some. "Do you truly believe they can keep our secret?"

"Yes, especially if they're in on the search. If you turn them away, I can't say what they might do."

He stayed quiet while considering that.

"I suppose we could cover more ground with their help," Seth said.

"And Gertie will let us know if anyone is nearby," I said. "Also, she likes Fritz and knows his smell."

He nodded his approval.

~ ~ ~

Sammie had brought cheese sandwiches which she shared out once we had gathered together in the spring house to hear what Seth had to say.

"That's good and tasty," he said. "Thank you." He spoke with his mouth full and somehow that bothered me. Of course Mama had drummed into me that a considerate person chews with their mouth shut. A bit of food fell from the corner of his mouth on the side where he seemed to have little control.

Sammie turned away with a sour look. Seth didn't seem to notice.

"Rex has told us that the Will'ven't Bin is somewhere near Browns Creek," Seth said, "in a small valley surrounded on three sides with steep hills. I have a map of Nashville."

"So, we're on a treasure hunt?" Sammie asked.

"You could say that," Seth said. He pulled from his haversack a folded sheet of paper coated with wax, and spread it out on the floor. We all knelt to get a good look.

As he pointed them out, I recognized the creek and a few roads in my neighborhood.

"I made the grid in blue grease pencil to help me organize my search," Seth said. "You see the squares with the blue lines through them? Those are places I've already explored without finding anything. If we search the rest of the squares carefully, I'm certain we'll find what we're looking for."

"When Daddy and I searched farmers' fields for Indian relics," I said, "we kept about 20 feet apart."

"That's smart, but we're looking for bigger things, so we'll space ourselves about 50 feet apart," Seth said. "That way, we can hear each other easily and there will still be an overlap of what we see. We must try hard not to miss anything. If you think you overlooked something, look into it, even if you think you've been to that spot several times already."

"How long will we have to search?" Buddy asked.

I thought he worried about missing his dinner.

"Are you tired already?" Seth asked.

"No," Buddy said, "just asking." Embarrassed, he looked down at the floor and didn't ask anything else.

Seth's lips pinched in and he shook his head. "I'm sorry, little fellow. I don't know how long this will take."

Buddy nodded.

"We're supposed to go with Mama and Daddy to the library benefit tonight," Sammie said, "so we'll have to get home in time for that, at least."

"What happens at this benefit?" I asked.

"People perform whatever they're good at, singing and dancing, magic, acrobatics."

"Sounds fun."

"It can be a little scary," Buddy said.

Sammie laughed.

"Enough of that," Seth said. "Let's get back to our plans."

"What are you after in the Will'ven't Bin?" Sammie asked him.

The left side of Seth's face churned with emotion and we all pulled back from him. I thought he'd got angry about the change of subject.

Then, he seemed to be struggling to focus on Sammie, blinking his eyes a few times and rubbing them with a hand.

Instead of showing anger, he grew silent for a moment, as if collecting his thoughts. "With your hair cut so short, I did not see that you're a girl." He got a wistful look. "My Clara—" A moan choked off his words. A look of anguish took hold of the left side of his face. He shook, looking down, tears dropping from his eyes.

We looked at each other and I could see Buddy's and Sammie's confusion. I'm certain they saw mine. I could only guess that Clara was a girl Seth cared about, maybe a daughter.

He wiped his eyes and took a deep, rattling breath. "Nothing in particular," he fibbed.

I didn't challenge the lie.

"But I have two reasons to find the Will'ven't Bin," he continued. "The first is that the Bin is filled with wondrous inventions. Some, in the right hands, could benefit all of us. The second reason is to keep those things out of the hands of Rex and his crew. I worked as part of their operation for a time. No matter what he says to the contrary, Rex does not have others' best interests in mind. He preys upon the fears of his followers in order to take and hold power. He is a flea, a mosquito, a leach."

"A parasite?" Sammie asked.

"Yes," Seth said, "Thank you."

"Why do people follow him?" she asked.

Seth gave her a crooked, sad smile. "Sweet girl, you shouldn't have to know about that."

"And still, I *want* to know. *And* I'm not *just* a *girl*."

Seth gained a lopsided smile. "My daughter, Clara, was a tomboy like you."

"I'm no tomboy," Sammie said. "That's insulting. A fake boy?" She stood up and stomped both feet with a short hop, raising a cloud of dust. And what a fierce look on her face!

Seth reached into his back pocket and pulled out a worn, stained wallet. "I didn't mean to insult," he said as he fished out a photo and held it up. The picture showed a cute little girl peeking at us from beneath a mop of brown curls. "Truth is, you remind me of why I love her."

Sammie backed down and sat, her eyes glassy looking. "You haven't told me why people follow Rex," she said softly.

And again, Seth seemed to collect his thoughts. We waited patiently. He put the photo and wallet away.

"The hurt inside them makes them vulnerable to his scheming," he said slowly, the trouble he had finding the right words plain to see. "Many, like me, are veterans of the Great War who have suffered. Some, like me, were wounded and have a much harder life now than before. Some, like me, because of what we did and saw in the war got a sickness of the head that makes us hard to get along with. We have spells now and then, becoming suddenly fearful or angry for reasons unclear to others. Things remind us of the nightmare we endured and the feelings come unbidden. We can't control it. No one will hire someone like that. Unemployment is higher among veterans. Many of us also lost our families with the change that came over us."

"I think my cousin, Harold Timmons, had that sickness when he came back from the war," Sammie said. A tear ran down her cheek. "He killed himself two months ago," she said, her voice and face aquiver.

I'd heard from Buddy that, even though he stayed sad all the time, Timmons had been good to the Cordell children and that Sammie had grown strong feelings for him. I'd never seen her cry before and I itched to do something for her. Nothing I thought of seemed like something she'd allow.

"Sweetheart, I'm sorry," Seth said.

"I'm not your *sweetheart*," she said bitterly.

Seth sat back, rubbing his face. "I simply want you to know I understand."

"What does your Clara have to do with any of this?" Sammie asked in a shrill voice. Her eyes grew wide and she clapped a hand over her mouth.

"That's none of our business," I said quickly, fearing she would get us into trouble.

Sammie dropped the hand. "That wasn't nice of me. I apologize."

"No, that's okay," Seth said, "I'll answer." He sat up straight, looked Sammie squarely in the eye. "Because of the war, I lost my health, my family, and my job at the paper mill back in Virginia where I come from. Of my family, I miss Clara the most. Angry over all that, I joined Rex's crew. He says he's organizing veterans to create his own army, and that once we have enough people and what's in the Will'ven't Bin, we'll be able to take over and give Americans a better life. I believed all that tommyrot until I couldn't any longer. With time, unable to stomach what he did, I left. Now, I want to stop him."

I couldn't pretend to know how to stop something like what Rex had going, but I knew that would take a lot of doing. Even so, I had to ask, "Why do you want to stop him?"

"He hanged a friend of mine at that odd fishing camp you talked about. A black man who saved my life in France during the war."

Sammie reached for Seth's spotty right hand and he let her lift it. With the sores on his skin, I was surprised she did that. She could be squeamish.

"I'm sorry you lost so much," she said, quickly wiping away fresh tears.

Seth merely nodded.

I saw a lot in Sammie that day that I'd never seen before.

Chapter 8

We all agreed to meet at the McClanahan spring house at nine o'clock the next morning. I meant to get there before everyone else and dig up that fish-shaped piece of green flint to see if the drawn image had changed again. While that seemed important at the time, I couldn't have explained why.

I took Seth to my "fort" in the woods, a place Mama had never seen, across the dirt road from my house. Daddy had helped me lay its foundation of gravel and bricks. I'd made the small room from used building materials I took from waste piles at construction sites. Having a tin roof, the fort stayed fairly dry.

I figured Mama wouldn't look for me there because one day, when Daddy and I wanted to show her fossils we found in the bedrock of the creek, she'd said, "I'm not going in those woods. Too many chiggers and ticks."

I looked over the place to see if anyone had broken in since last I'd been there. The small windows remained latched from the inside. The padlock on the door had not been forced. Standing within a woods choked with underbrush and vines, the fort wasn't easy to see from the road. I don't know who owned that property, but as far as I could tell, they didn't use the land for anything. Lots of small and large woods in the area were similar mysteries.

Using the moon's light, I got out my key and let us in. Inside, I took a candle lamp from a wall shelf and lit the wick. That small amount of light would not be easily seen from outside unless one stood close to the fort.

I had two musty-smelling sleeping bags hanging from the ceiling that we took down and used for the night. Musty or not, they felt fairly dry and comfortable.

"Tell me about war in the trenches," I said, lying down on my bag and resting my head on my shoes. "Was it like camping out?"

"No," Seth said flatly, "nothing pleasurable about it. You don't want to know."

"Yes, I do. Some of what you saw and did had to be exciting."

Seth turned on his side facing me and propped his head on his hand. "I'll tell you about trench rats," he said.

"Okay," I said, hiding my disappointment.

"At the front, we slept in below-ground bunkers within the trench system. While rats thrived on the death and destruction all around, they made us ill, and those illnesses sometimes turned deadly. They got in our food and fouled it with poop and piss. They nested and bred wherever they might stay fairly warm and dry. Even in new sections of trench, there were quickly more rats than soldiers." Seth paused as if to see what I thought.

I reckoned he hadn't given me much, so I had nothing to say yet.

"Rats are most active at night," he continued. "They moved around in the dark where we couldn't see them. They ate our dead and the animals—mostly horses and dogs—killed in battle and lying scattered across no man's land."

"I've heard all about no-man's-land," I said stupidly.

"Have you, now," Seth said. "Well, you may know all about the war already. Why should I waste my breath?"

"No," I said. "I just know what I've heard from friends and class-mates. You know the truth."

Seth stayed silent while I watched him.

Finally, I said, "Please."

He nodded with half of a half smile and kept quiet a bit longer, no doubt to punish me for being a know-it-all. Then he spent what seemed like five minutes clearing his throat before speaking again.

"The rats ate our candles so we had little light in a world already blackened with despair. Rats even tried to eat lit candles, sometimes toppling them and starting fires. They crawled on sleeping soldiers and often bit them. Some of the men had a hard time resting for fear of being bitten. Some feared being eaten alive in the night by a pack of rats. The constant presence of the rodents drove men mad. Our only satisfaction came with the rains, when rats drowned in the trenches. They couldn't climb up the slick sides and get out of the rising water. We made sure not to help them. Drowning rats was the only good thing about the rains. Already a quagmire, the trenches just got muddier still. With all that wetness, our feet never dried out and we got trench foot."

"That's enough about rats," I said.

"What's wrong," Seth asked, "you don't see the glory in all this? Isn't that why people go to war, to earn glory?"

"Tell me about no man's land."

He lay back, looking at the tin ceiling. "I can't, but I started to talk about mud. What if I tell you about that?"

"No, tell me what it's like to take a man's life. Did you kill anyone?"

"Yes." Seth said, closing his eyes. "You make the war sound like a grand adventure. In truth, I found myself bored most of the time. A lot of waiting, watching, listening, preparing, and then waiting some more. I got the idea that my superiors made our time that boring so we'd be willing to risk everything for a little excitement."

"What about when the enemy attacked?"

"Oh, sure, that happened on occasion. Sometimes the enemy would show up and try to shoot us. Other times, we had artillery bombardments or gas. And sometimes we had to rise up out of our trenches and run stupidly across no man's land toward the enemy trenches."

"Stupidly?"

"Stupid because we died in great numbers trying to take territory that had suffered complete destruction. And to what end? Even if we took territory, the enemy took it back within a few days."

"We won the war, didn't we?"

"No, we didn't win anything. The enemy lost the war."

"What does that mean?"

"I cannot explain well enough for you to understand."

He had a lopsided, angry look. What had I done? He'd turned against me for some reason. Or was he having one of his spells? Would he become angry and violent like he did on the day he kicked Fritz?

"So now I'm too dumb to comprehend?" I'd used the ten-dollar word I'd learned from Daddy hoping Seth would think me smart. That didn't work.

"You are an ungrateful child, you know that? You want to borrow my wartime experience, even when I'm certain you see I suffer just talking about it. Compared with most of the folks around here, you've had it good at home with your Mom, yet you ran away from that. Yes, you are an ungrateful child."

"She doesn't treat me well."

"Does she feed you and give you a warm place to sleep?"

"Yeah, I guess."

"Sounds like she's done most of what a good mother should do. You have to do the rest."

"I lost my father and she treats me like—"

"She lost your father too. You think she's had an easy time? Having spoken with her, I know she's sick with worry over what might happen to you. She's doing her best while feeling the same hurt you are. The fact that you are ungrateful tells me you have had it good. Don't feel too bad—most children are like that until they grow up."

He no longer looked angry. Maybe he'd calmed down.

"She wouldn't let me go looking for Fritz."

Seth kept quiet for a time. Finally, he said, "Well, no one should come between a boy and his dog. I can understand your need to find him. She shouldn't have tried to stop you."

"So I'm not ungrateful?"

"Oh, you're still ungrateful. You've had a good, soft life. You wouldn't have lasted a minute in the trenches."

He'd said that to hurt my feelings, I felt certain.

"Could be that's because I'm just twelve years old." I said with a huff.

"Don't listen to me, boy. Don't you know I'm embittered?"

I fell silent and he watched me.

After a time, he spoke quietly. "Your mother paid me for working on the hedge stumps even though I didn't finish the job."

"How much?"

"Two bits."

"You didn't work five hours. Three at the most."

"She's a nice woman. How much she chose to pay me is not truly any of your business. I tell you merely so you'll know it's part of her character."

He'd found an argument I couldn't challenge.

"Tell me about your friend that Rex hanged," I said.

He kept quiet for so long that time, I thought he ignored me. I'd dozed off a bit when his voice awoke me.

"William Stowbridge—"

"Yeah?" I said quick and eager.

"—belonged to the 369th infantry regiment of the U.S. army, known as the Harlem Rattlers. The American commanders didn't believe that blacks could be relied on in a fight, so the 369th had labor instead, far from the front lines, stuff like laying rail lines and unloading ships.

"The French were used to blacks fighting alongside them and they needed the replacements, so the Harlem Rattlers finally got to fight. They fought so well, the Germans called them 'Hellfighters.'"

"Replacements?"

"Men to replace the dead or wounded."

"Makes them sound like machine parts."

He nodded. "In 1918, I met William in the Argonne Forest in northern France. He'd gotten separated from his regiment. Lost in the night, he stumbled into our bivouac during a German assault."

"Bivouac?"

"Not trenches with bunkers. In this case, an unsheltered camp with fox holes in a ravine where we'd become trapped, surrounded and cut off from reinforcements."

"You mean your allies?"

Seth nodded. "When he showed up, William had so much mud on him, none of us knew he was black. Thinking he might be the enemy, someone tried to shoot him. He dropped into my fox hole and the shot missed.

"Two German soldiers appeared up above us on the eastern side of the ravine. I could scarcely see them in the dark. Just silhouettes with muzzle flashes as they fired at us. My magazine exhausted, I said quietly, 'Reloading.'

"William fired on those huns. They would have had me if he hadn't. One fell forward against a tree stump and stayed that way. The other tumbled down the hill and came to rest with his face in the creek at the bottom of the ravine.

"The threat gone for a short moment, William gestured toward the north, then swung his hand around eastward until it pointed south. 'Mine,' he whispered. By that, I knew he wanted me to defend against any threats on our western side. Each of us having a section of the compass to defend, we fought off the attack all night, and, on and off, for five more days. Although few words passed between us, an understanding grew: We fought for each other.

"Once our commanding officer discovered William was black, he tried to remove him from our ranks, even whilst we were cut off. A good thing he didn't succeed. We needed every man.

"On the sixth day of being surrounded, our forces broke through and the fight for the ravine ended. Starving from lack of victuals, suffering a powerful thirst because German snipers had kept us from getting water from the creek, and with our weapons useless for lack of ammunition, we walked out of there."

"What's a sniper?"

"Soldiers with high powered rifles with magnifying scopes that allow them to shoot something very far away. You don't see them, so you don't know a bullet is coming. If it's your time, that can be a blessing of sorts, I think."

I tried to imagine being desperate enough to fill a canteen at a creek while someone tried to shoot me.

"Holy cow, what a story," I said, "You and William are heroes. Wow!" Truly, I did not know what else to say.

"After the war, I visited him in Harlem. We became good friends."

"I don't know any black people," I said. "Not well, that is."

He nodded his head. "When I came south to Tennessee, he came with me. I could tell Rex and his crew didn't respect William. I had no idea they'd lynch him for looking at a white whore."

"You mean a strumpet?"

He frowned. "Where'd you get that word?"

"My daddy."

"Yes, one of a few strumpets Rex had brought in to entertain his men."

I thought about the library benefit Sammie had spoken of, with its talent show. "You mean she did a performance of some kind?"

"You could say that."

The longer his story went on, the quieter and more hoarse his voice had become. Now just a whisper, I wondered if that hoarseness came from damage to his throat from the mustard gas.

I smiled for him. "You gave me a real war story, after all. Thanks. I'm awful sorry about your friend."

Seth rubbed his head and face, like he could remove the memories that way. "Don't smile too big," he said. "If there's another war, you might get shipped off to the fight. It's not what you think."

Why did he say that? Had he turned off mean again?

Seth took something out of his pocket. Watching him rub the thing with his thumb, I recognized the green piece of flint.

"Hey," I said. "That's mine."

He looked at me curiously, but otherwise ignored my words.

"May I see that rock?"

He held the stone up in the dim light. The piece of flint having the same fish shape as the one I'd discovered at the spring house, I knew he'd stolen it. "Where did you get it?"

"I picked it up off the ground in France during the war. It's my lucky charm. It hasn't felt good in my hands lately, so I hid it. It seems to quiver a bit when I touch it. I can't say it ever did that before. I'm trying to get used to it." He eyed me in a way that made me uncomfortable. "Did you find it in the floor of the spring house? Are you the one who drew on it?"

"Maybe," I said stupidly. His cloudy gaze had rattled me.

Seth held the stone out for me to see it in the light. He pointed at the near-perfect rectangle. "I scratched that into the stone with a knife during an artillery barrage that went on for so long, some of the men went mad. Not wanting that to happen to me, I concentrated on making the best rectangle I could. I imagined the lines were walls to keep the war and what it might do to me away from the other parts of my life."

"Must have dulled the blade. That's hard stone."

"Dulled it so badly, I couldn't sharpen it well enough later and had to get a new knife."

He jabbed at that rectangle again. "I trapped 1918 in there. You put another rectangle over mine. Yours holds 1933. That star is me. I truly do not know what will come of it."

He sounded upset.

"How is that star you?" I asked pointing. "I put the dot there."

"I made it a star."

"And how is *that* you?"

I don't know how I know. I just do. Even if you scratched it there, that glowing dot feels like me, trapped between the years 1918 and 1933."

"That's an odd thing to say, odder still that you had the thought."

"Not everything makes sense," he said with a huff, his words full of disgust. "Some things you know in your gut. Took me a while to understand that. You'll see for yourself one day."

That sounded like nonsense. I considered the possibility that the sickness he'd spoken of had made him think like that.

Yet hadn't I believed I'd communicated with dead Indians? I kept that to myself.

Seth looked like he was trying to move one of the rectangles cut into the hard stone. Why he thought he could do that, I don't know, but he seemed to succeed in making the rectangles match up, one exactly over the other.

Deep booming off to the east caught our ears. The sound wasn't much like those that came from the train yard. Then I heard a flat popping that sounded like distant gunfire.

Seth, in a panic, rubbed at the stone until the rectangles separated.

The booming and gunfire ceased suddenly as if a door had been closed. "Sorry," Seth said, looking like a little boy who had done something wrong. "I didn't mean to do that."

"Did you move one of those rectangles?" I asked.

"I don't know what you mean. They are scratched into the stone. You said, yourself, the stone is very hard. You can't move the rectangles." A twitching around his mouth told me he might be lying.

He shoved the piece of flint back in his pants pocket, slung an arm across his eyes and turned on his side, facing away from me.

Moments later, he cried out, "Ah-ah, no! Get it off!" Seth wriggled on his sleeping bag, brushing at his face, and crying out, "Get it off."

I saw what upset him: A daddy longlegs crawling on his mangy scalp. Snatching the bug from off his head, I showed it to him.

"And here I was thinking you're one tough fellow," I said.

"I don't like spiders," he said most pitifully.

"Daddy longlegs aren't spiders." I tossed the bug to the wall beside me and it hurried away, leaving behind that odd smell they make.

Remembering what Seth had said about the soldiers fearing rats in the night, I couldn't help adding, "They do sometimes come in swarms to feed. You better hope they don't swarm over you in the night and eat you alive."

Saying nothing, Seth turned away from me again.

And, once more, I had to realize that the scariness of the small creatures, even in a swarm, couldn't compete with the nightmare of the trenches.

I blew out the candle and lay still, trying to sleep. Took some time to get there because I got the ridiculous notion that rats watched me as I lay in a darkened bunker.

Chapter 9

The next morning, Seth had little to do to get ready for the day since he'd slept in his clothes. He sat rubbing the sleep off his face, while I hung the sleeping bags up and dressed.

I'd considered allowing him the use of the bathroom at home, but he smelled so bad, I decided he'd make too big a mess and I didn't want to spend my time cleaning.

"If I can get in the house," I said, "I'll get some of Daddy's old clothes for you."

He gave me a lopsided smile.

We hid in the underbrush by the road, watching my house and waiting for Mama to leave. Must have been mid-morning by the time she went out. She carried a sack with her. Could be some of her anti-macassars sold and she was on her way to deliver more. I remembered the big smile on her face the first time she'd sold one to a neighbor. With the hope that gave Mama at the time, I couldn't help feeling happy for her.

Just a day before, I wouldn't have cared why she left the house or where she went. I wouldn't have thought about whether or not she was happy. Now, though, something about hearing from Buddy that Mama had been crying while looking for me and Seth calling me ungrateful had me trying to put myself in her shoes. I realized that after Daddy died, I had mostly ignored her, concentrating on my own suffering instead. Even if we weren't much alike, I had not been there for her as much as I might have been. I'd need to make up for that. I decided that once I found Fritz and went home, I should be a better son.

Once she'd walked out of sight down the dirt road, Seth and I went to the house. A window in one of the basement light wells had a loose latch. He helped me pry up the sash, breaking the latch free.

Seth hid in the hedge. I went inside and up the stairs. In the guest room, I opened some boxes where Mama had stored Daddy's clothes. She meant to sell what she could and give the rest to charity. Seth appeared to be about Daddy's size. I figured he deserved charity, like any other unemployed, homeless person. Having been so harmed in the war, maybe he deserved that kindness even more.

I picked out two pairs of heavy trousers, one brown, the other gray, a couple of gingham shirts and a gray fedora. Along with that, I took a pair of gumboots Daddy had worn when we explored the creek and caves, a couple pairs of socks, and underwear. From the hall closet, I pulled out a carpetbag that had belonged to my grandparents and loaded the clothes and boots into it, then a bar of soap from the bathroom and a grocery sack from under the sink in the kitchen.

The fedora on my head and carrying the carpetbag, I went down the stairs from the kitchen to the basement and back outside the way I came in, closing the window behind me.

Dirty as the glass looked, I didn't think anyone on the outside could see through the window well enough to know that the latch had been broken. If Mama didn't look up at it while in the basement, she might not notice either. I'd fix it once Fritz and I were home again.

"That hat is too big for you," he said. "Did you get it for me?"

"Yes." I offered him the fedora.

His eyes got big. He took off his old, threadbare flat cap, stuffed it in his back pocket, and donned the newer hat, spending some time fiddling with the crown and brim.

"A little large on me," he said, "I can fix that with some folded paper."

"Looks good, but pull the brim down more in front"

Seth nodded and tugged on the broad felt rim.

"Let's see what else you got," he said.

"Let's go back in the woods first."

Following me across the road, he said, "Tell me, then, what you got."

"You'll find out soon enough," I told him.

Once back in the woods, he looked like he expected me to hand over the clothing right away. I tried to ignore him as we picked our way through the trees and underbrush.

"Fresh clothes are no small thing," he said, sounding a little embarrassed. "Mine are stiff with sweat, and the odor brings back bad memories."

"Until now, I haven't seen you eager for anything except the Will'ven't Bin."

I took the bar of soap out of the carpetbag and handed it to him.

"I'm sorry you've had to put up with my smell."

"I just hope the clothes I brought fit. If they do, you should keep them."

"Thank you. I'll bathe before I dress."

At the creek, he pointed at a leafy tree limb that draped low over the moving water, said, "If I get under that, I'll have some privacy."

I gestured toward a hollow log at the water's edge. "I'll put the clothes there so you can choose what you want to wear."

He took off his worn-out shoes and got in the water under the overhanging limb. With the leaves hiding him, he undressed and took a quick bath.

I spread the clothing out on the log and put his shoes and old clothing in the grocery sack, figuring they could be washed and worn again.

Waiting for him, I sat on the end of the log, which slowly collapsed under me. A redheaded skink dashed out of the hollow and scampered away through the weeds. I got up and leaned against a tree, watching soap bubbles from Seth's bath flee downstream. Some got trapped in little eddies near the steep creek bank, where they spun around and around, going nowhere.

I couldn't help seeing myself in that—here I sat, beside the same creek, going nowhere. What possible future did I have? How long would we suffer such unemployment? Would there be jobs for me when I needed one?

I'd once had a dream of being a soda jerk. Yes, I liked sweets, but I'd been drawn to all parts of the job: the smells, the gadgets, all the shiny glass, the colorful syrups, candies, ice creams, and the antics of the soda jerks, themselves. They added a flare to every move, whether tossing ice cream into a cup or jerking a fancy soda spigot to fill a glass, they danced their way through the workday, usually with some jazz music playing on the radio in the background. I loved it.

Thinking of what Seth had been through, I decided I should not feel sorry for myself. I still might make my dream of becoming a soda jerk come true.

Finished with his bath, Seth said, "hand me a pair of those boxer shorts, the green shirt, and brown pants."

I did and moments later, he came out from under the overhanging limb in his shirt and shorts. He climbed up the bank, hid himself in the underbrush, and finished dressing.

The brief glimpse I got of more of his skin told me the mustard gas had scarred him all over.

"The shoes are a little loose," he said.

"Wear both pairs of socks. I can always get more."

Once he'd dressed fully, we walked downstream along the creek, passed under the old stone bridge at Caldwell Lane, and moved on to the McClanahan spring house where my friends, Sammie, Buddy, and Gertie waited.

Chapter 10

We sat in a circle on the floor inside the spring house. Sammie handed out baloney sandwiches. "So, what's the plan?" she asked.

"Since Daddy and I struck up friendships with many of the local farmers," I said, "I might easily persuade some of them to allow us to search their woods. They're used to me and Daddy searching their fields for stone points, but I'll say we're now looking for burial mounds. I figure some won't know my father died. With Seth dressed like him, if he stands far enough back while I go to the door, they might think Daddy is the one asking through his son."

"You mean your father making you talk, even though he's dead?" Buddy asked.

We all stared at him. I didn't know how to answer that, and no one else seemed to either.

"Wouldn't that scare them?" he asked, his voice trailing off toward the end so we could scarcely hear him.

Sammie huffed. "Yeah, like you were frightened of that ventriloquist dummy speaking at the library benefit last year."

"That wasn't real," Buddy said.

"You thought it was," she said, laughing. "You're so gullible."

Buddy turned red. "He won't be there this year," he said as if reassuring himself.

"Enough," Seth told her. "No, son, that's not what Martin means. They won't get scared." He patted Buddy on the shoulder. "You are full of wonder, aren't you, boy."

Buddy smiled. He kept quiet for some time.

"While standing back a ways and wearing the hat," I said to Seth, "keep your head down and wave at them when they come to the door. If any of them know Daddy passed away and question me, I'll say you're my Uncle Seth, Daddy's brother, that I'm introducing to amateur archeology."

"If they call me to their door to talk," Seth said, "I'll have to come right away. To hesitate would be to draw suspicious. As I'm approaching, tell them what mustard gas did to my skin and eyes, so they won't be too surprised seeing me up close."

I nodded.

Seth got out his map and spread it open.

"What are the new marks in red grease pencil?" I asked.

"I've been adding information to the map based on recollection of those parts," he said. "Those are communicating trenches." He pointed at different lines and symbols. "Those are—

He turned to me, a look of irritation on the left side of his face. "Wait a minute, you don't need to know that. If you got captured—"

"Seth, are you thinking about the war?" I asked.

He looked confused for a moment. Sammie and Buddy scooted away from him a little, worry on their faces.

Seth's hands began to shake. He shook his head fast, blinked a few times, and said, "I'm all right. I know where I am."

"And where is that?" Sammie asked gently.

"We're in Tennessee," he said. Although he remained seated, Seth placed both hands on the dirt floor, maybe to steady himself.

Sammie reached out and squeezed his left hand. He gave her a weak smile, his breath hitching some.

~ ~ ~

Once we had talked over our plan, we set out to search the first empty square on Seth's map. Most of the forested area in that square covered low hills on the western side of Browns Creek. The nearest farm, about fifteen acres, belonged to Deke Franklin, a white-haired, old man who lived alone in a rough, one-room cabin. He raised pigs and feed corn. He'd let Daddy and me search his fields. I didn't think he knew my father well.

Boy, did I get that wrong.

When Mr. Franklin answered our knock on his door, I introduced Sammie and Buddy.

"Who is the fellow out there?" Mr. Franklin asked. "Is he with you?"

Seth stood about fifty yards away in the gravel drive that led to the house. The way he'd asked that, I could tell Mr. Franklin felt threatened. I didn't know why.

"Oh, uh…, that's my Uncle Seth."

"Your mother's brother, then."

"No, uh, Daddy's."

Mr. Franklin stepped back, looking like he didn't know what to make of me.

"You are Martin Thompson's boy, aren't you?"

"Yes."

"Your father was an only child."

I had to think fast. "Oh, uh, in truth, he-he's not my real uncle," I said loudly—Seth needed to hear what I said of him so our words would agree.

"Well I swan, young man—no need to shout. I'm old. I ain't deef."

I gestured for Seth to join us. "He-he's my father's best friend from college. I always called him uncle. Seth served in the Great War. Mustard gas harmed his skin and eyes. He stood back like that because he doesn't like to startle people. I'm introducing him and my friends here to amateur archeology."

"Good morning," Mr. Franklin said as Seth walked up.

"Good morning to you, sir, I am Seth Knopes."

"I hope you understand about me being careful," Mr. Franklin said. "There have been raids on several farms in the area from groups of hoboes. They started with farms folks had abandoned after banks foreclosed. Once they cleaned them out, they turned to the rest of us. They come in the night and take anything they can carry away."

"Do you have anything to protect yourself with?" Seth asked.

"Yes," Mr. Franklin said, "if it comes to that. But, enough unpleasantness."

He looked at me. "I knew your father even when he was a tyke. Men with his powerful curiosity don't come along every day. Too bad we lost him."

"Thank you, sir," I said. "That's a fine thing to say about him."

Mr. Franklin turned back to Seth. "I understand you fought in the Great War."

"Yes, sir," Seth said. "Luckily, Martin Senior avoided that."

"Well, good of you to serve. I'm sorry you got injured. The least I can do is allow young Martin here to show you what he and his father loved so much."

"Thank you, sir," Seth said. Slowly, he extended his hand to shake Mr. Franklin's. Could be he moved so carefully because he thought he might be refused. Mr. Franklin took the hand right away, without looking at it.

"You folks have fun, now."

We all thanked him.

He went back inside and shut the door.

~ ~ ~

Three times during the search, Seth crouched, cringing when he heard railcars coupling in the train yard nearly a mile away. I quietly explained to Sammie and Buddy that I believed he was suffering bad memories of the war from that sickness he'd spoken about. Buddy shrugged. With a sad look, Sammie bit her lip.

Stupidly, I thought that if I were harmed, maybe she'd have feelings for me too.

Late in the day, Buddy complained, "Are we just searching in circles? All of this looks so much alike." He looked tired.

"Not to worry, young fellow," Seth said, "I'm keeping track of where we've been and where we're headed."

Sammie turned to Buddy and said, "We should go home for dinner and to feed Gertie before the library benefit."

"Let's meet up again at the spring house at nine o'clock in the morning," Seth told them.

They agreed.

"Where is Gertie?" Buddy asked.

"She knows the way," Sammie said. "She's hungry, so she's gone on ahead."

Soon as the word, "hungry," left her lips, Gertie appeared out of the underbrush, bounding toward the two.

"Yes," Sammie told the dog, "we're coming."

They turned away and walked off into the trees.

~ ~ ~

Dusk had fallen, making our search that much more difficult. Now just the two of us, Seth and I talked about quitting until the next day.

We'd entered a hollow between two steep hills. Moving through thick undergrowth, we stuck to trails foraging deer had made.

"Let's do this gully before we quit for the night," Seth said.

Passing between the hills without finding anything, we came out at the edge of farmland. We stood beside a fallow field that recent rains had turned to mud. A farmhouse sat about a hundred yards away to our right.

Hearing the sounds of one or more people moving through the forest behind us, we crouched, ready to run.

"That might be the enemy coming up on us," Seth said, gripping my right forearm too tightly.

I thought he meant Rex's crew. The voices kept getting closer.

He pointed at a cut about forty yards out in the field that must have been for irrigation. "We should get to that trench."

Keeping low, he ran out into the field and I followed. Immediately, my shoes were mired in mud and my steps became heavy. We got to the irrigation ditch and crouched low.

"Keep your head down," he said. "There might be snipers."

I believed he meant Rex and his men had such rifles.

Night had arrived, a dark one at that moment, since the moon hid behind clouds. Smoke curled from the chimney of the farmhouse and a dim orange glow could be seen through the curtains of one window.

A chicken coop sat under what looked like a giant burr oak behind the house. A scattering of lightning bugs flashed yellow-green in the gloom. Even though the air stayed warm and sticky, I shivered, my heart racing.

The voices, now sounding like a bunch of drunkards, headed toward the chicken coop. One man with a flashlight had a dog on a leash. The dog whined and pulled the man toward us.

"That's the fellow I saw with Rex," I said, "the one in the gray suit."

"That would be Colonel Shufflewell," Seth whispered. "Colonel in title only, not military."

The dog barked and I recognized the greeting. "And that's Fritz," I said, and lurched forward to climb out of the ditch.

Seth grabbed me and pulled me back down.

Colonel Shufflewell jerked on the leash that held Fritz. The dog whined and leaned forward, straining against the tether to get to me. The man, his eyes on what Fritz did, hadn't noticed us.

"War dog!" Seth whispered. "You don't want that to get a hold of you. Run that way." He gestured in a direction that followed the line of the ditch.

"No, you said you'd help me find my dog. That's him. That's Fritz!"

"The Colonel might have a pistol. He could kill you. Now, go!"

I knew Seth spoke the truth. Still, I dithered. "I can't," I said gesturing at my clay-caked shoes.

"You should have let me tell you about mud. Shake your feet, damn it!"

I did. Much of the mud fell away.

"I see you, Seth," Colonel Shufflewell called out.

Man and dog were almost upon us when I heard old squeaky hinges, and looked toward the farmhouse. A back door had opened and a man with a shotgun came out.

Did he wear a uniform or was he a farmer?

Colonel Shufflewell turned toward the farmhouse.

The man with the shotgun fired his weapon, and Shufflewell cried out. He turned quickly and started back toward the woods, having to drag Fritz with him.

"Now run!" came Seth's urgent whisper in my ear. "Pretend your feet are wearing big shoes and get moving."

I tried, stumbling forward through the mire.

Glancing back, I saw the shotgun fire toward the chicken coop.

Someone else cried out in pain.

"You've had all the free eggs you're gonna to get," the man shouted in a heavy accent, possibly French. "Now, clear off my property,"

The voices near the coop became an excited jumble, moving back toward the woods; someone moaning, another laughing, and some angry cursing.

I fell. Hitting the ground forced a sound out of me.

"Quiet," Seth said. "Aw, hell, he's coming this way. Get up and run, damn it!"

The man with the shotgun had indeed turned and now moved in our direction.

We ran as best we could. I heard him fire again and saw the shot pelt the ground at the lip of the ditch ahead.

Seth grabbed me across the ribs, pulled me up and off my feet like I was a piece of luggage. We turned a corner at the end of the ditch and entered a small stream that must have fed the irrigation when flooded. Seth put me back on my feet.

Eroded and steep, the creek bank rose behind me. We waded through the water along the edge in a northerly direction, which would take us back into the woods.

The shotgun went off again, the shot striking near where we'd entered the creek. I looked back and saw the silhouette of the man with the gun in a swirl of mist. He stood on the bank about thirty feet away. I could have sworn he wore a military uniform of some sort. Since night had fallen, the darkness kept me from being certain of that.

Shaking, Seth murmured words I could not understand.

A flash of light close to the horizon, then a crack and deep rumble. Thunder?

As if hearing my thoughts, Seth said, "No, that's artillery."

He crouched beside me in the water up against the bank and crossed his arms over his head for protection. The water had undercut the clay of the bank in that spot, leaving an overhang that helped hide us.

Still, I could see the man with the gun. He aimed in our direction. I pushed my back against the bank. The gun went off again.

Seth got a piece of shot in his shoulder. He stayed down, whispered. "Keep quiet."

More flashes, deep rumbling, and the loud cracking sounds drawing nearer. A deafening explosion up on the bank outlined a tree in white light. Branches and twigs fell into the creek.

"Mortar fire," Seth said. "They're adjusting, trying to find us. Maybe they'll hit the guy with the trench gun first."

Seeing drowned rats and dead soldiers floating by in the creek, I panicked and tried to climb up the bank. Seth gripped my thigh and held me down.

He leaned out to look again. "That fellow must also think the mortars will find him. He's leaving in a hurry."

When Seth let go, I put everything I had into climbing. Because of the overhang, I couldn't get up and kept sliding back.

I made one last great effort to get to the top of the bank and my foot hung on something. Kicking the thing free, what looked like a long bone went flying from the clay. I started sliding down again. Trying to grip anything that might stop me, my hands dug into the bank, and the smell of clay filled my head. I touched something solid and gripped it. Sliding farther down, I held on, and the thing came out of the clay in my hand.

A human jawbone! I could see the worn and broken teeth. Startled, I let out a short cry. Seth looked up as I tried to figure out where the bone had come from. A skull peeked out at us from a hole I'd made in the bank.

Seth must have seen that too. He picked me up again, stepped over the fallen branches, and ran along the creek bed like it was a nice, flat trail. He didn't stumble once.

Eventually, we came to a wooden bridge. He set me on my feet and we climbed out and up to find a dirt road.

"There are patrols that will find us if we tarry."

We crossed the bridge and headed in a northeasterly direction along the road.

"I've been back here a few times, but I've never dragged anyone with me before. I thought it was all in my head."

He meant the war, I felt sure. He'd confirmed my worst fear.

Then the rain started, fat drops striking the top of my head, knocking sense into me.

~ ~ ~

I woke up in the fort, scarcely remembering that we had found our way there in the night.

Seth still slept.

Daylight came through gaps in the walls, telling me we'd slept late.

The sense knocked into me the night before had not left. I knew my imagination had run away with me. There were no soldiers, dead or alive, no rats, no trenches, no artillery or even trench gun, just a storm with thunder and lightning, a farmer with a shotgun, and a bunch of pilfering hoboes, Rex's crew. The air had a crisp, electric something-or-other left over from the storm.

I had to get away from Seth. He didn't live in the same world I did and that made for problems I couldn't handle.

Without awakening him, I slipped out of the fort and went home.

He'd called me an ungrateful child. Thinking about how he'd helped me find out what happened to Fritz, I felt the truth of that. Even so, I knew I should stay away from him. As far as I knew, he didn't intend to harm anyone but Rex and his crew. If I kept avoiding him, he'd get the message over time.

Chapter 11

My three nights away from home had brought about a miracle. Mama wept when I showed up about noon. She fell to her knees and hugged me so tight, my ribs ached.

"I'm sorry. I am not proud of the way I treated you," she said. "I know you love your dog so much you had no choice but to run away from home to find him."

Although I liked that she could see my side of things, she filled my left ear with loud sobs and her tears soaked the shoulder of my shirt. I gently pushed her away. When she looked at my face, I gave her a smile.

Suddenly, she had my right hand in hers as she pulled me into the dining room and made me stand next to the big windows where she'd have good light. Mama looked me over, tears still growing in her eyes.

"You are unharmed." She looked surprised.

Shaking the tears off, her manner changed. "I should punish you severely for the way you made me worry."

"Okay," I said.

She seemed to ignore my willingness to accept punishment. "I have too much going on now to have to worry about you too," she said.

Strange that I'd felt much the same way when dancing to her tune.

Then her manner became pleasant again. "Did you find your dog?"

"You mean *Fritz*."

She gave me a knowing look.

"No," I lied.

"With time, he'll come back," she said, sounding like she thought that a good thing.

Following that, the lecture started. I listened politely, my head bowed and my eyes down. She talked about her role as a parent and my need to be "considerate."

I wanted to smile and chose not to. I didn't know why I should. Could be I felt happy to be home after all that had happened.

At some point, much quicker than with past lectures, she ran out of wind. I expected one of her weak spankings or some other kind of punishment, yet none of that happened.

She made oatmeal for us for breakfast. I loaded it up with butter and brown sugar. While we sat eating, she said with a big smile, "I found a job."

I dropped my spoon and it bounced off the table and fell to the floor. Mama bent to retrieve it.

"Great news!" I said, glad to have been wrong about her willingness to find work.

She gave me the spoon and I continued eating.

"I'm bagging groceries at the A&P, Seth's old job. That's just a start. I hope to rise to better positions with time."

"That's wonderful, Mama."

"Not with your mouth full…"

"Sorry."

She smiled. "In fact, I'll be late for work if I don't leave. I have no time to clean up the kitchen. Will you be all right on your own?"

Could that be the reason I got such a short lecture? No, she seemed genuinely happy to have me home.

"Knowing I've been away on my own for a few days, you just looked me over and said I'm fine."

She nodded and smiled. "Well, I suppose I must trust you. Try not to burn the house down. If you go anywhere, stay out of trouble. If it's not too hot, please mow the lawn."

Trust? Would she? Something had seriously changed in her. I could only hope that change would become permanent.

"Yes, Mama. Before I can mow, I'll need to find the file and sharpen the mower's blades."

She took up her purse from the sideboard in the dining room. "Oh, my lunch." She returned to the kitchen and grabbed a brown paper sack from off the table. "There's pimento cheese in the icebox. You can make a sandwich for lunch. I'll bring home something for dinner."

And then she left, walking out the front door and down the dirt road toward town. I watched her go, feeling relieved to be left on my own again so soon. If she'd known what I meant to do, she would've tried to stop me.

Still hungry, I made a sandwich to take with me, wrapped it in wax paper, and shoved it in my pocket. I left the house to get to the Cordells' place before Sammie and Buddy would leave to make our nine o'clock meeting at the spring house.

By then, I'd forgotten all about mowing the lawn.

I arrived to find my friends eating. Mrs. Cordell answered my knock on the kitchen door in her gardening apron. The kitchen table held a mess of dirt, pots, and African violets.

"How do you do?" I asked her.

"Fair to middlin,' thanks," she said. "And you?"

"I'm okay. The real news is that Mama got a job. She's bagging groceries at the A&P."

"Oh, my, she has succeeded where so many others failed. Good for her."

Sammie and Buddy sat in the dining room, eating their breakfast. I don't think they so much as looked up upon hearing the news. That didn't bother me. Thankfully, they had been protected from most of the hardships others had been forced to dealt with.

"We're having a late breakfast because of Buddy's piano lesson," Mrs. Cordell said. "Are you hungry?"

"I have a sandwich," I said, pulling it from my pocket.

"That looks a bit wadded up."

"I don't mind."

"Get a plate from the cabinet and have one of those apples," she said, pointing to a bowl of the fruit on the dining room table.

I did like she said and sat with Sammie and Buddy to eat.

After the two finished with her eggs and bacon, Sammie said, "Let's go to Buddy's room."

Her mother gave her a look. "When have you ever wanted to go in Buddy's room?"

"We're planning a surprise you can't know about," Buddy said.

Sammie eyed him funny. I don't think their mother saw that.

I put my uneaten apple in my pocket and followed the Cordell children.

In Buddy's room, he showed me the plans for our next electrical tower model.

"This will be the most complicated one we've made," I said.

"Yeah, but we can do it, right?"

"Of course."

When he nodded, seeming to automatically accept that, I realized that he often looked to me to know what was possible. I saw that as possibly dangerous for him, especially lately. That gave me an uneasy feeling. I should be protecting my friends from the dangers I'd been finding, instead of leading them straight to them. Still, I needed help to get Fritz back, especially if Seth were no longer involved.

"We should not meet with Seth anymore," I said.

Sammie looked surprised, so I told them much of what had happened the night before.

Wide-eyed, Buddy asked. "Did anyone get killed?"

"I don't know," I told him. "Rex and his guys are that dangerous, so I wouldn't be surprised."

"You're okay, though, right?" Sammie asked.

"Yeah, even if my imagination went to town on me."

"Are you saying you made up some of that story," she asked.

I hadn't told them about the rats and the dead bodies in the creek, and the things that Seth had said about trenches, artillery, mortars, war dogs, and trench guns.

"More like things didn't mean what I thought they did?" I said.

They looked confused.

"I don't know," I said, frustrated. "It was dark, and a lot happened I didn't expect. There are things I know now about Seth that make me worry. He sees things that aren't there and thinks he's back in the war. When that happens, he can be violent. I know it sounds funny, but his bad thoughts are, I don't know, contagious maybe."

"You believed you were in a war?" Buddy asked.

"A bit." I said, unwilling to admit more.

"Do you mean you thought you had to fight?" Sammie asked.

"No, and I had no weapon to fight with, anyhow. I began to think Seth had brought the war here, to Tennessee. Even if he conjured up the visions, though, he did save me from harm last night."

"You had visions?" Sammie asked.

"Yes. I mean, no. Okay, so I think I could have been seeing things too, probably out of fear. I just don't know what to expect around Seth now and I think we should steer clear of him."

"What harm?" Buddy asked.

"A man with a shotgun—could have been a farmer—chased after us and I fell. Seth picked me up and carried me to safety. He got a piece of buck shot in him for his trouble."

"But he's okay?" Sammie asked with a worried look.

"Yes."

"A good thing he saved you," she said, "If he's crazy, though, you're right, we should stay away from him."

She placed a hand on my forearm. Her touch felt so good and warm, I feared I'd completely fallen for her, something that made me a bit queasy.

"I wouldn't say he's crazy," I said. "His own pain makes him act like that."

"Then that's it. I hope he'll be all right." Sammie looked sad.

"I'm sorry," I said, pushing down on the weird feelings. "I know you had *something* for him because of your cousin, Harold Timmons."

She looked embarrassed. "Not like you're thinking!"

"There's nothing wrong with having a kind heart."

"Of course not. It's just that, of all people, I don't want *you* to think

I have a crush on him."

Why me? What did she mean? That got me thinking she had feelings for me, and the queasiness returned.

"Hopefully, he'll get better," I said. "Even on the day we met, he'd said things I found threatening. I also came here to be away from home so he wouldn't find me right away. At least he doesn't know where you live."

"What'd he say that was threatening?" Buddy asked.

"He questioned me to find out if I'd seen any junk yards in the forest. That day, even though he hadn't told me about the Willa'ven't Bin yet, I think he tried to see if I knew something about it. I said I didn't know what he was talking about, and he said he'd get answers out of me eventually. The look he had as he said that scared me."

"He's sick," Sammie said. "He doesn't know what he's doing."

I wasn't so sure about that.

We left Buddy's room and returned to the kitchen. Mrs. Cordell had cleaned up most of her repotting mess.

"Before you go out to play," she said, promise me you'll be home by six for dinner. Martin do you want to join us?"

"No, thank you, Mrs. Cordell. Mama expects me for dinner."

"Are we going somewhere?" Sammie asked me.

"No, I need to go home."

Mrs. Cordell turned away to finish cleaning up the kitchen.

Sammie gave me a questioning look.

I gestured toward the door and she followed me out.

"See you later," Buddy said.

"Bye."

Once outside with Sammie, I said, "when you said, 'Of all people, I don't want you to think I have a crush on him,' what did you mean by that?"

"Well, you are my boyfriend, right?"

"I am?"

Seeing my surprise, she laughed.

"You're my friend and a boy, aren't you?"

She teased me, that's all. Sammie had somehow seen my feelings for her and now used that against me. She wasn't older than me by just a couple of months, but a little over a year. For a short time every winter, she became two years older than me, if only in numbers. Because of that and her smarts, she'd always have the upper hand. I had to wonder if I could take that. I had the answer immediately, a frightening one. That and the teasing got me upset.

"I came to tell you those things," I said quickly, "so even if you went to the spring house, you'd know I wouldn't be coming to the meeting." Then I spun on my heels and stomped off, feeling like a jerk as I realized the grass of the lawn kept my heavy footsteps from showing my anger.

"If you go home, Seth will find you there," she said with a giggle.

I wanted to strangle her.

I wanted to kiss her.

So confusing.

"Yes, he'll find me," I called out over my shoulder. "I can't hide from him forever."

"What about Fritz?"

I didn't answer her question. I hadn't said anything about seeing my dog with the man in the gray suit, Colonel Shufflewell. The best thing would be for Fritz to come home on his own, since I didn't want to risk the dangers of going to get him. Still, I figured I'd have to do that. If Rex's hoboes found him useful enough to take on one of their raids, like they'd done the night before, the poor dog was probably kept on a leash so he wouldn't get away.

Chapter 12

I returned home in the late afternoon.

Seth stood beside the back door of my house. I had to wonder how long he'd waited there.

"You ran off on me, son." he said. "And after I helped you find your dog. You are *indeed* an ungrateful child."

"I got scared," I said. "What we did last night put us in great danger. We could have been killed."

He nodded his head. "I'm sorry about that. I didn't mean to take you there."

Again, I thought he meant the Great War when he said "there." I remembered him saying the night before, "I've been back here a few times, but I've never dragged anyone with me before. I thought it was all in my head."

I'd told Sammie I didn't think Seth crazy. Even with that, I had the feeling his losses and suffering had driven him a bit mad.

"I need your help," he said, "I'll take that help by force if I have to."

Looking into his cloudy eyes, I knew that if I got twenty feet away from him, I'd be mostly beyond the range of his vision. He'd still be able to see me, yet not well. If I ran, I would likely lose him. That did seem ungrateful. Of course, he'd probably called me ungrateful so I'd have doubts. I did feel bad about not wanting to help Seth. I couldn't decide whether or not I owed him. Although I meant to stop helping him, I wanted him to understand why. "I cannot win in a fight with Rex and his men. I don't want to die at the age of twelve."

Seth hung his head. "Doesn't matter. I need you."

I took a step back.

He reached into his haversack. Dropping it and lunging at me, he took my arm in a painful grip with his left hand. He spun me around so that he held me from behind. I felt the chill of his trench knife against my neck. "I would rather not hurt you," he said.

I believed him, and decided to pretend to give in and help. At the first chance, though, I'd ditch him. That might force Seth to treat me even worse. I'd deal with that when the time came.

At first, the thought of the Will'ven't Bin had filled me with wonder. Then, when Seth had told me about the time machine, I'd seen a way to be with Daddy again. Now, considering the trouble that had come with knowing about it, I wanted nothing to do with the Will'ven't Bin. In fact, I wished I'd never heard of it.

"How do you know the Will'ven't Bin hasn't already been raided?" I asked.

"If there's the slightest chance the time machine is there, it's worth everything, even if I have to harm you. With it, I can get back to my family, and get my job and health back. Hell, I could start over as a young man."

Having had the same idea for how to get back to Daddy, I understood. Still, stuff had gotten out of hand. Too many dangers.

"That may be," I told him, "but if you go back, you'll likely keep memories of what happened in the war. And if that's true, you have no reason to think your body and mind will be healed. Wouldn't you be taking who you are now with you?"

Standing there, holding me, Seth stayed quiet for too long, maybe thinking about what I'd said. His grip loosened a little.

I wriggled suddenly and hard. He tried to tighten his grip. I got my head and left shoulder out from under his left arm and jammed my right elbow hard into his gut. He coughed raggedly, let go, and fell to the ground, holding himself and continuing to hack.

Mama rounded the corner of the house at that moment. Her eyes got big and she hurried to Seth's side. She helped him sit up and pounded him on the back. His hacking had a wet sound and he spit on the ground. I saw blood and something yellow-green in his spit.

Crouching beside him, I said, "Seth, are you all right?"

"No," he said simply.

"Let's get him in the house," Mama said.

Mama took his upper body, and I lifted his legs. Even so, we dragged him some going inside. We put him in the guest room, which hadn't been opened since shortly after Daddy died. The air inside, hot and musty, held a hint of mildew. The afternoon sun shone through the windows, throwing beams of light through swirls of dust we'd stirred up. The boxes of Daddy's things, full of mostly books and clothing, had been stored on the floor and stacked against the walls. That left thin aisles for walking around the bed and dresser. As Mama bent over, helping me lower Seth onto the bed, she upset a stack of boxes and they tumbled onto the floor. Out of one spilled an Army/Navy Surplus haversack. The mud crusted on the heavy kaki canvas told me Daddy I had used the sack exploring a cave.

Once in the bed, Seth turned on his side and closed his eyes.

I stacked the boxes back up and placed the haversack on top. Mama pushed the curtains aside and opened the window.

I'm not sure why I decided not to tell her about Seth threatening me with his knife.

"What are you doing home?" I asked.

"I had an appointment with my doctor and got off early."

"On your first day?"

"Don't think the world here stops when you're not around. You were away for some time. This wasn't my first day. My boss is an understanding fellow, don't worry."

"Are you all right?"

"Yes, I'm fine." She placed a warm hand on my shoulder, said, "Nice of you to ask."

"What are we going to do with Seth?"

"Dr. Engler makes house calls. I'll go to Sylvia's and ask to use her telephone."

She went out. Through the sunlit dust and the open window, I saw her walk across the back yard, push through the gap in the hedge, and disappear into the Westlake property.

I sat on a chair next to the bed. Seth turned so he could see me. "I'm sorry for scaring you, Martin."

"You can't help being ill."

"No, not for this here spell I'm in now. I'm apologizing for trying to force you to do what I want. You're not an ungrateful child. You are just a child, like all other children. I should not have mistreated you. I am the ungrateful one. My only excuse, if you'll have it, is that I've lost everything and simply want to start over again. If I get to, I'll act better, I promise. But I fear I'll die before that happens."

"You're not going to die."

"I think I would know more about that than you do. And, as you pointed out, I am what I am, no matter the date. In some ways, it's a relief to know I won't have too long to wait. At the same time, I would have dearly loved to see my Clara again, even if I remained ill."

Although Fritz and I had suffered at his hands, Seth's words brought a tear to my eye. How had I allowed that? Maybe something to do with the way he'd spoken to me and how Mama got his old job because he'd told her to try for it. I had truly warm feelings for Seth for the first time. What he'd done to me and Fritz had come from the hurt he had inside. I could forgive that.

"I wish you had not drawn on my lucky charm," he said. "That changed everything."

He must have seen my confusion. "The piece of flint you drew a dot and a rectangle on," he said.

He chose that moment to worry about a rock? Yes, I thought, he'd surely gone mad.

"I reckon you're going after your dog now without my help, aren't you?"

"Yes."

"I know I cannot dissuade you, so I won't try."

"I don't want you to tell Mama."

"I won't."

"Thanks."

Seth took my hand. "Listen to me now. Approaching their camp, wear clothing the colors of the forest. If you get winded, breathe through your mouth. Don't shuffle your feet. Lift them a bit higher when taking steps and walk with your knees, elbows, and back bent slightly, hands out to the sides a little for balance. That way your muscles are ready for whatever comes, especially changes on the ground that you may not see through the underbrush. For each step, plant your foot on its side, then roll onto the heel. Glance at the ground enough to avoid encumbrances, while keeping your head and eyes up as much as possible, looking and listening for movement on all sides. Take heed of more than the nearest sounds. Freeze if a sound makes you suspicious."

"Okay, okay!" I said, pulling my hand away.

"All that will make you a lot quieter, less noticeable."

"Yeah, if I can remember what you said."

He gave me a one-sided, sad smile.

"Thanks," I said. "I'll try."

"And keep in mind that your dog will smell you coming."

~ ~ ~

After dressing, I went back to the guest room. Seth appeared to be asleep. I took the WWI haversack from off the stack of boxes and moved through the house quickly, loading into it a few things I might need: My compass, a canteen, strike-anywhere matches, bandaids and aspirin, two sandwiches, some treats for Fritz, a ball he liked, and his leash.

In the hall by the front door, I stopped to look at the fine, glass-fronted barrister's book cabinet Daddy had gotten to hold and display our relics. Light from the small, high hall window lit the interior nicely. Along with the best stone points, we'd included other types of Indian relics we'd found: The heads of tomahawks and axes, stone chisels, pottery, implements made from shell, and stone balls that Daddy suggested were for playing a game of some sort. And of course, we also included in the cabinet our sloth fossils, civil war relics, and, with their permission, some of the Cordells' best finds. I'd been meaning to see if all that needed cleaning, but the Oklahoma that settled everywhere else still hadn't gotten inside.

Though lost in memories, I did hear the kitchen door opening. I barely got out the front door as Mama came in the kitchen. Not knowing if she'd heard me leave, I ran across the front lawn and the dirt road. I entered the woods and headed upstream along Brown's Creek.

I heard Mama behind me in the growing distance, calling for me to come back. Hopefully, she would understand that I still hadn't finished my task of bringing Fritz home.

A quarter mile up the creek, winded from all the running and feeling the heft of the haversack, I realized I should have emptied the thing before putting more in. The sack held equipment Daddy and I had taken on our last spelunking expedition and weighed more than I wanted to carry. Even so, I wasn't willing to dump it out.

Later, I'd be glad I hadn't emptied that haversack.

Chapter 13

I'd made it past the odd fishing camp and stood at the edge of Rex's community. Fritz's bark, instantly recognizable, came from ahead, maybe a quarter of a mile away. Hadn't Seth warned that the dog would smell me coming? I shouldn't have been surprised. Fritz didn't try to give me away. He simply wanted to be with his pal.

Quickly, I looked to find the tree I'd hidden in before. No luck, I climbed one that held a thick grapevine.

What a stupid decision! Colonel Shufflewell came into view with Fritz leading the way and five men trailing them. My dog led them straight to me. I did my best to hide among the leaves and branches.

"If it's not a squirrel," Shufflewell said, "it might be Seth or someone else wanting to make trouble. Surround that tree," he said pointing roughly in my direction. "Look for an intruder!"

The men spread out to do his bidding. Shielding their eyes from the bright, white sky, they searched the leaves and branches.

Fritz whined and jerked against the leash that held him back.

"Hush!" Shufflewell commanded, and smacked him on the head.

Single-minded in his desire to get to me, Fritz didn't flinch.

"There," one of the men said. He pointed right at me, though I had ducked back behind thick clusters of leaves. "Give me the shogun," he said.

I looked about for an escape. Big loops of the grapevine hung between my tree, a walnut, and another nearby, a red oak. I leapt for a loop to climb hand over hand to the oak. With rapid cracking and popping, the vine started to tear loose from the branches above and I began to fall. Those sounds trailed off and my falling slowed. All but one stout branch of the vine had let go, while I had kept my grip. Suddenly the vine and I swung free toward the oak. When close enough, I hooked a leg over a branch. I let go the vine, and got my other leg and arms wrapped around the limb.

Hanging upside down, I blinked to get bark chips out of my eyes, then looked down again. Someone handed a shotgun to the man waiting for it. I scrambled to pull myself up and over the top of the limb.

A glimpse of the fellow raising the gun sent me leaping for another branch. I grabbed hold with my arms and swung to its other side, where another nearby limb, a stout one running parallel to the first and a bit lower, gave me a surface to stand on.

The shotgun went off with a loud crack. Chunks of bark went flying from the limb, exposing the wet, reddish wood inside. I could smell the sour, skunky sap.

Keeping my balance, I walked along the limb, coming close to the foliage of a nearby maple. I leapt for a limb in the maple, hoping it would support me. The branch bent with a cracking sound. I hung from its underside and went hand over hand toward the tree's trunk, where the branch would hold my weight better.

Once surrounded with maple leaves, I heard the men below questioning what had happened to me. I couldn't see them. I heard Shufflewell's blustery voice just before he caught up with the rest of his men. "Climb that maple," he said.

I looked for an escape, saw above me that one of the maple limbs had cracked where it met the trunk and slouched into another tree. Since the branch went the direction I needed to go—away from Rex's community—I climbed up and slid down its length, tearing my pants and painfully scratching the insides of my thighs. I ended up near the ground in another oak.

"He's there," someone said.

Not waiting to see who and how many, I hung from the low-lying limb and dropped to the ground. Fritz's barking and the angry voices of the men calling out gave me some notions as to where they were.

I heard the contents of the haversack—brass carbide lamps—rattling against one another as I ran. On our last expedition, Daddy and I took them with us to explore Antioch Cave by boat. Unlike flashlights, carbide lamps don't mind water and they make a brighter light that lasts longer than something with a battery. I feared the sound would give me away, even if those chasing lost sight of me. Again, I wished I'd emptied the haversack at home before putting in more. To stop the sound, I unslung the thing from my back and hugged it tightly to my chest.

I recognized parts of the woods I'd passed through and knew I would come upon the creek soon. If I got across the water, that might confuse my scent trail enough that Fritz would lose track of me. I hit the water running, sending spray everywhere. The rocks jutting up out of the stream got spattered, and I knew that those chasing would easily see that and know the direction I'd gone.

The sound of the men chasing me came louder with each passing moment.

The straight course I'd taken had done me no good. They could run faster, but being smaller, I figured I had the advantage of agility. I zigged and zagged through the trees, looking for spots to hide.

So frustrating, the haversack still made noise, a smaller rattling sound. I almost tossed it into the underbrush, yet I didn't want to lose those carbide lamps since they had belonged to Daddy and me.

Pretty soon, I saw hills ahead, then rock outcroppings among the trees on a slope to my left. With hope of hiding among the rocks, I changed course. That seemed to throw off those chasing me.

Of course, Fritz got them right back on track. If only he knew how he helped them and what they might do to me!

I saw a dark opening among the rocks ahead, and ran in that direction. That's when I thought of what made that smaller rattling sound: Our can of carbide rocks! If the darkness ahead turned out to be the opening to a cave, I'd be in luck.

I got up the slope and moved around until I could see what I'd spotted from below. Yes, an opening!

The thought that there might be a dangerous animal inside always occurred to me as I approached a new cave. This time, I also had a fear that I would be entering a shallow, single-room cave with only one way out, allowing Shufflewell and his men to easily capture me.

The ceiling, a great slab of grey limestone, sloped down at a steep angle from one side to the other. I ducked quickly inside, turned and, from a crouched position, searched the foliage outside for movement. There, a short distance away, small, leafy limbs jerked this way and that—the men were coming up the slope.

I turned and moved deeper into the cave.

Crouching, I got a carbide lamp and the canteen out of the haversack. The weight of the canteen told me I'd forgotten to put water in it. Damn!

Hearing dripping water in the distance behind me, I knew my luck hadn't run out. I shoved the lamp and canteen back into the sack and headed toward the sound, sliding my feet forward carefully, feeling the floor to avoid stumbling or falling into a crevice. My hands out, I felt along the wall to my right. I got to an edge, where the stone dropped off toward the floor. Beyond that, the cave opened up enough that I could stand straight. I could not find the far wall at first.

Muffled voices from outside made their way to me. I stood as still and quiet as I could to hear better.

"Did you know this was here?" someone asked.

"No, anyone else?"

Several "nos."

"Get in there and find that boy," came Shufflewell's voice.

"We have no torches or—"

"Go back and get a couple of those squeezy flashlights," he said.

Again, something I'd seen at the Army/Navy Surplus store, I knew that to be a type of light powered by hand squeezing a part of the mechanism.

I moved slowly toward the dripping sound, feeling my way. Hearing the carbide stones rattling softly inside their metal container, I couldn't help thinking about the hardship of my last outing with Daddy. We'd had to abandon the boat, which sank, and swim out of Antioch Cave. Standing outside, dripping wet and shivering, I got so cold, I thought I'd never warm up. I hoped never to suffer that again, but seeing how hard Daddy laughed at our failure had made the expedition worthwhile.

Then his laughing stopped suddenly and his eyes got big. "Are you all right, Martin?"

"Yes, Daddy," I said, my teeth chattering.

He hugged me, giving me some of his warmth. As he pulled away, I said, "A little longer, please? I'm s-so c-cold."

He wrapped me in his arms again.

"I hope Jessup won't be too upset with me for losing his boat," he said.

"He told us it was on its l-last leg," I said. "He w-wouldn't have loaned the boat to us otherwise, right?"

"Of course you're right."

"I-I dropped the haversack in the water."

"I grabbed it before it sank to the bottom." He pointed to where he'd dropped the sack on the ground once outside the cave.

"What about the carbide?"

"The can is watertight and the lamps don't care. All we have to do is empty and rinse them out."

I'd found the source of the dripping sound. Opening the haversack, I took out the can of carbide rocks and a carbide lamp. I pulled open the cap to the lamp's reservoir and held the opening under the drip until I could feel the water overflowing. I wiped the lamp down with my shirt and set it on the dirt floor at my feet. Using the dull side of my pocket knife blade, I popped the top off the can of carbide. I reached for the lamp, unscrewed it midway to get to the hopper, which I loaded with carbide, then screwed the parts back together. Turning the lever that allowed water to drip from the reservoir into the hopper, I heard and felt the reaction inside: The rocks, coming in contact with the water, released acetylene gas with a slight burbling, the pressure in the hopper building. I could only hope the tip was clean enough to let the gas out. In the dark, I'd never be able to get the tiny cleaning wire into the hole in the lamp tip.

A quiet hissing told me that nothing clogged the tip. I used my thumb to rotate the wheel on the flint striker to get a spark. The tip made a pop as the flame, at least three inches long and brilliant white, lit my surroundings. Using the lever on the reservoir, I adjusted the size of the flame to make it a little smaller, and set the lamp down.

I held the canteen under the drip and stood waiting for it to fill up, all the while itching to move on before the men from outside returned with their squeezy flashlights. When done, I screwed the cap back on, returned the canteen to the haversack, shouldered the sack, and picked up my lamp.

Now, I hoped the cave had enough passages that I could confuse my path and lose those following me.

Chapter 14

Black arrows appeared here and there on the cave walls, likely meant as a guide back to the entrance. Looking much like the ones Daddy and I drew on the walls of caves we visited, they were no doubt made of carbon given off by the flame tip of a carbide lamp. The arrows did not point back the way I'd come. That told me the cave had more than one entrance. Unwilling to go back and risk getting caught, I moved in the direction the arrows pointed.

I wondered if I stood in a cavern Daddy and I had visited that I just didn't recall being in the area.

No, this one had huge stalagmite and stalactite formations that I'd never seen before, like great dollops of slowly dripping peanut butter. Though I knew better than to think they might fall, I cowered down when passing beneath the largest formations. I figured Daddy hadn't known about the cave or we would have explored it together. Being larger than most in the area, that would have taken several expeditions.

If the men chasing me got those squeezy flashlights and entered the cavern, I didn't hear them.

I moved through a couple of passages so tight I feared getting stuck, dodged my way through one filled with columns of stone, and came to a ledge high up along the wall of a gigantic room that echoed the sounds of my movement. Peering over the edge and down, I tried to see the floor. The light from my lamp didn't reach that far.

Across a four-foot gap, stood a series of giant broken stones, a jagged ridge made of what looked like formations that had fallen from the ceiling. The light of my lamp didn't reach the ceiling when shined upward. Peering into that darkness, the silence pressing down on me, I felt terribly, uncomfortably alone. At the same time, I also feared running into someone.

I had to make a leap across the gap to the broken formations. Preparing myself, I knew I could easily jump farther than four feet, but because of the stone columns behind me, I couldn't get a good running start. The smaller broken stones across the gap had been pushed to the sides, so I figured I still followed the well-worn path.

I made the hop across and landed firmly. Standing and taking my next step, I knocked loose small stones and slipped. My right leg went out from under me and I toppled to the right, grabbing a broken column of stone as I fell. Having enough weight, the stone held me, even though I'd rocked it loose from its resting place. Dizziness gripped me and I lay on the path, my heart pounding hard until my head cleared.

With time, I grew calm enough to get up and move on. I made my way across the "ridgeline" of broken formations and into another passage on the other side of the giant room. Here the smooth wall curved away from me above and to my right. Glistening with water droplets, the stone looked like a great, sweaty brow.

I entered another, much smaller room that had a crevice running down the middle of the floor. Above, the ceiling teemed with bats. Disturbing their poop underfoot, the ammonia odor of bat guano rose to my nose.

The walls, also sweaty-looking, narrowed. I moved forward, at first straddling the hole in the floor. The ceiling angled downward, forcing me into the crevice and deeper. I saw a floor about fifty feet below.

While climbing down, I heard a moan that sounded like someone in pain. I wanted to call out, yet didn't want to give myself away. When the voice came again, I had just stepped down onto the floor. The sound seemed to have come from somewhere along the passage ahead. I crept forward, placing my feet for silent walking the way Seth had instructed, then realized that the glow of my carbide lamp had probably already given me away.

"Hello," I said, keeping my voice low.

"Help," came a weak response from about fifty feet away.

I could not see anyone in the passage. Shining my light upward, I saw blood on the wall to my right, about twenty feet up.

"Are you hurt?" I whispered.

"Y-yes. Can you help?"

"I'll try."

The passage curved to the left, and to the right. Making the second turn, I found the man, Lawrence, that I'd overheard talking with someone named Ned on the day I discovered Rex's community. Lawrence lay on the floor, his left shoulder and head against the wall. He didn't look in my direction. Had the voice truly come from him? As the fellow stayed completely still, his face turned away from me, I had to wonder if he had given up the ghost. Had the voice come instead from somewhere farther up the passage?

I crouched down, leaving a couple of feet between us. "Can you move?"

"Not much without it hurting," he moaned.

I must admit, having thought him dead, his voice startled me that time.

Figuring he couldn't hurt me easily, I moved closer, and panicked when he gripped my hand. I held down my urge to get up and run.

His breath came in gasps and hitches. "They threw me down here from above. My right hip is broken, maybe the lower leg too."

Quaking with each word, Lawrence looked at me curiously and frowned. He let go my hand suddenly, said, "I reckon you're not one of Rex's. So who are you?"

Seemed to me more like he *hoped* I wasn't one of them.

"I'm Martin. I'm looking for my dog, a German shepherd named Fritz."

"Do I hear water sloshing?" Lawrence asked.

I offered him the canteen from my haversack.

He didn't reach for the water. "If you don't mind... Moving is painful."

I held the canteen for him as he drank deeply.

With his slight movement, I noticed blood puddled beneath him. He had a long tear in his right trouser leg and a wound running up that thigh. Reminded me of ones I got on my forearms from falling off Buddy's bike. I'd hit a big hole in the road out front of his house. The front wheel broke and I went over the handlebars. Sliding arms first on the paved road removed a lot of skin, and sure did hurt.

I got out my bottle of aspirin.

"You think *that* will help?" He sounded angry and disgusted.

"Couldn't hurt," I said.

He allowed me to place two tablets in his mouth. He chewed, and I gave him water to wash them down.

I screwed the cap on the canteen, put it aside, and took one of the sandwiches from the haversack.

His eyes got big. "I'm so hungry!"

I tore away the wax paper to get to the sandwich and started feeding him.

"Try not to speak loudly," I said. "Somebody we don't want to find us might hear."

Chewing, he nodded.

I unwrapped the other sandwich and started eating.

Although I'd immediately thought his disloyalty to Rex had gotten him there, I had to ask, "When and why did they do that to you?"

"At least a day ago, perhaps more." Lawrence said with his mouth full. "I've been lying here in the dark for so long, I don't really know." He swallowed and gasped for air a bit. "Do you know of a man named Rex?"

"Yes," I said, "I've never met him."

"My cousin, Ned, belongs to Rex. He got in trouble, stealing liquor. Giving me up as a traitor got him off the hook."

I gave him more sandwich.

"I overheard you talking with Ned two days ago."

He looked at me curiously, yet didn't say anything. I think he was surprised to hear I'd been so close to the lion's den, so to speak.

"You two didn't know I was in the tree above you. Ned said something about Hoover and troops shooting at veterans. Did he mean the president?"

"Yeah, we were part of a demonstration," Lawrence said, "trying to get our wartime bonuses early. There must have been close to forty-thousand of us veterans and family members living in a shanty town we'd set up across the river from the capital. Most of us had no work and the bonuses are not due until 1945. The government was never going to give us the bonuses early. The army drove us off with tanks, tear gas, and fixed bayonets. At least two veterans died in the assault."

"That's terrible. I didn't know. I'll bet that's why Hoover didn't get reelected."

"Yeah," Lawrence said with disgust. He'd clearly had enough talk of history. "Do you know the way out?"

"I have an idea, but may have to search some. You're not going anywhere on those legs with a broken hip. I'll have to get out and send help."

"W-will you do that?"

"Yes."

Tears fell from his eyes, making fresh tracks through the dust on his sweaty face.

"I believed I'd die," he sobbed. "Lying in the endless dark, I thought I had died."

"I'm sorry. And here I am, about to leave you in the dark again." Do you have another light I can use?"

"No," I lied. "Selfishly, I didn't want to risk losing the spare lamp. "I'll be okay."

"Can't go out the way I came in. Some of Rex's men might still be at that entrance. I have to follow the arrows on the walls to find another way out."

"I don't know the passages well enough to help you."

"That's okay. I'll be gone for several hours probably. I *will* come back, I promise. Can you wait here quietly?"

"I don't have any choice. I do have hope, at least, thanks to you."

Though clearly painful for him to do so, he gripped my hand

again."

"Hopefully, I'll find an arrow somewhere along this passage," I said. We had finished our sandwiches.

I filled the reservoir of my carbide lamp with water, then left my canteen with him, got up, and walked along the corridor.

"Be careful," he called out as I passed around a bend and he must have lost sight of me.

~ ~ ~

I saw an arrow pointing downward toward the end of that passage. Getting closer, I saw a hole in the floor. Daddy had called such tight, vertical passages "chimneys." Passing down through twists and turns about thirty feet, I came out in another big room. I heard shuffling sounds and voices, muffled with both echoes and distance.

To my left, I saw a wooden pipeline like one I'd seen while with Daddy at Indian Grave Point Saltpeter Cave. About 80 miles away, that was the farthest we'd traveled from Nashville for an expedition. Hank Cordell had taken us there in his Marathon automobile. Sammie had gone with us. Buddy had remained home because he'd gotten sick with chicken pox.

I believe that had been the day I fell for Sammie. She'd had no problem with the dark, the chill, the mud, or getting her clothes wet and dirty. Her legs being too short for her to straddle a crevice we had to climb down, Hank had rigged her up with a rope so she could rappel to the floor. She'd performed like a champion, and I'd became so impressed with her, I lost some of my assumptions about what girls could do. What did I know about females, anyway? On that day, in my eyes she'd suddenly grown prettier, smarter, and stronger.

Turning the flame down low on my lamp, I moved forward, creeping around the left side of a giant shape that looked like a tree growing out of the floor. The trunk, about five yards across at the base, disappeared into the darkness overhead. Actually made of stone and larger than any tree I'd ever seen, the formation probably hung from the ceiling. Graceful, stoney forms spread out like a skirt at the base to become shelves standing a little above the floor. Each shelf held odd-ly-shaped clear pools of water with thin walls between them. Small, round beads of stone, looking a bit like pearls, rested in clusters in the bottom of each pool. I'd never seen stranger formations, and I wished Daddy could have seen them. He might have been able to tell me how they formed.

Beyond the giant formation, the sounds of men working came more clearly. Above the workers, strings of electric lights hung from metal hooks fixed to the stone walls. How they got that powered, I don't know. Maybe the electricity came in from a steam turbine outside.

Must have been a hundred men doing different tasks. Some off to my right were digging with mattock and shovel, others straight ahead loaded what they dug up into—I don't know—hoppers or vats. Whatever they might be called, they looked to be old mining equipment, made of wood, and very old. Off to the left, a few men worked on the wooden pipeline where it emptied into huge metal vats, and several more looked to be building a new wooden vat.

Then the answer came to me: Using equipment probably left there since the Civil War, they mined saltpeter. Almost anywhere the floor was soft enough to dig, the dirt was mostly bat quano, which held lots of potassium nitrate, also known as saltpeter. Daddy had said they used to call such miners peter monkeys. These guys were making gunpowder! But why? Wouldn't smokeless powder do a better job?

Before someone noticed me, I needed to get out of there. I had yet to find a black arrow to guide me. Skirting the edge of the room, I came to another wooden pipeline. That one seemed to come from the darkness to the right of the giant formation I'd just passed. I decided the men digging on that side wouldn't notice me in the darkness, as long as I stayed quiet.

The floor had lots of small stones that caught my feet. I moved slowly until the floor seemed to smooth out. In a hurry, I sped up, stumbled over something, and landed with a loud "oof."

Looking back, I saw that most of those digging had stopped to look in my direction. I knew they couldn't see me. Still, their eyes tried to penetrate the gloom. Most went back to digging while a group of four broke away and started in my direction. The one in front had a squeezy flashlight.

In a panic, I got up and ran. Glancing back, I saw the four coming my way pick up speed. Although I held my lamp so they could not see its small flame, I'm certain they saw what light it gave reflecting off my surroundings.

And then I tripped and fell again.

I turned up the flame on my lamp, got up, and ran.

Shouting behind me and more off to my right. I rounded the giant formation, found the wall and the pipeline running along beside it.

There, where the pipeline took a turn toward the wall to my left, a small tunnel about half my height. Above the opening, a black arrow pointing up let me know that the opening could take me out. I crouched and slithered in beside the wooden pipeline, scarcely able to fit. I realized that those chasing me would have to think twice about crawling in. At the same time, I worried I might get stuck.

Like I'd thought, about ten feet in, the tunnel became too tight.

Looking back, I could see the legs of the four giving chase approach beyond the opening, then the squeezy flashlight shone in my face.

"Jackson, get in there and pull him out," the man with the flashlight said.

"I can't fit in there."

Water dripping from cracks in the pipe ran along the floor. I dipped my hand into the wetness and rubbed the spots where the rock and wooden pipe held me in place. Mixed with the dust that coated everything, the water made a thin film of slippery mud, just enough to grease me up. I wriggled until unstuck and went deeper into the tunnel.

"He's getting away," the man with the squeezy flashlight said. "Who knows where that tunnel comes out?"

No answer. I didn't wait. The tunnel opened up enough that I could stand. I trotted forward, hoping no one knew where I'd come out.

Chapter 15

Seemed like I walked about a mile and a half of uphill passage before the wooden pipeline took another left turn into a small breakdown. On one of the loose stones lying on the floor, I saw part of a black arrow. I had no way of knowing which way it had originally pointed. Could be the way out lay beyond the breakdown, but again, I had no way of knowing that.

The tunnel continued beyond where the pipe made its turn. I moved along that passage for some distance, and came to a section that held standing water. The ceiling angled downward, meeting the water ahead. I had to return the way I'd come and get back to the breakdown.

Once there, I began moving stones. Dust that had settled around and between them over the years had taken on dampness from the air, forming a weak glue of sorts. Some of the stones had become wedged in tight. I scraped away the mud, rocked the stones until they came loose, and removed them from the path one at a time.

Stopping to rest, I heard a muffled voice coming through the breakdown, then a tapping, as if something hard struck the rock on the other side again and again. A crack of light appeared in the wall of stones, and a shadow blocked that light for a moment.

A dim version of Sammie's voice came through the crack. "Martin, is that you?"

"Yes," I shouted. "Where are you?"

"I'm here, in the spring house." She worked at one of the stones at the edge of the crack of light. "We've got to get you out. Remove any loose stones you can."

I did and within moments we had a hole big enough for me to see her face. I'd never been so glad to see that troublemaker. Out of breath and red-faced, she said. "What mess have you gotten yourself into now?"

I could not have predicted I'd find my way by underground route to the McClanahan spring house. The twists and turns of the cave passages had completely confused my sense of direction and distance.

We had removed enough rock for me to squeeze through. When I stood in the spring house, brushing the dust from my clothes, Sammie pushed my arms aside, hugged me tight, and planted a kiss on my cheek.

"I'm sorry I made fun of you being my boyfriend," she said and released me.

I stepped forward and Sammie didn't budge, except to close her eyes. Her face close to mine, I gave her a quick kiss on the lips.

With that, I began to shake and feel puny. I turned away, thinking I might vomit and not understanding why I'd reacted to her that way. Knowing her well, I had easily accepted all the sides of herself she'd shown me over the years, and, somehow, she gotten prettier by the day. If I had a girlfriend, she'd be it. Luckily, I had nothing on my stomach to throw up.

"Are you okay?" Sammie asked.

I didn't want her to think my reaction had come from kissing her, even if that were the truth.

"Yeah, I'm all right. I've had a hard time—I'll tell you later."

She tugged on my arm until I went with her out of the spring house and into the failing light.

"How'd you know I'd be here?" I asked.

"I didn't. This is only one of the places I looked for you. I heard you making noises."

"I need to talk to your father," I said.

"Follow me."

~ ~ ~

In the kitchen of the Cordell home, as we sat at the kitchen table,

Hank listened to me patiently.

He had always been close with Daddy. A veterinarian, he had survived the crash of '29 well enough because of the demand for his services. He earned less and sometimes got paid in small livestock, butchered meat, or canned goods, but he remained busy. He had been the one to introduce Daddy and me to using the carbide lamps while spelunking.

When I'd finished my tale, he said, "I had no idea we had such criminals in these parts."

"Me neither," I said.

"Can we help, Daddy?" Sammie asked. "Should we go to the police?"

"Sammie, Martin just told us that this fellow, Rex, pays the police to look the other way."

"Oh, yeah," she said, looking embarrassed. "Well, do you know a doctor who would go in and help that man?"

"Most of the doctors I know well enough to ask for such a thing are too old to crawl around inside a cave. Besides, before he can be treated, we need to get that poor man out of there."

Thankfully, Mrs. Cordell had gone out, so he didn't have to consult her. Marjorie had always been more cautious than Hank.

"I'll have to think about how to go about it," he said. "If not done properly, Lawrence could die, not to mention the difficulties for whoever goes in after him. He'll have to be strapped into a rigid stretcher. Ropes can be used to lift him and the stretcher. Sounds like I'll need help—adult help—to lift him up through the crevice you described."

"Lawrence needs to know help is coming," I said.

"I can't do anything tonight," Hank said. "And you need to rest, young man. You should go home and show your mother you're okay. She came here earlier in the day, looking for you. Because Sammie had told me you'd gone looking for Fritz, I lied to your mother, saying you'd spent the night. I told her you were both out looking for Fritz."

"How did she take that?" I asked.

"She seemed to accept the fib," Hank said. He rubbed his face as if frustrated. "Let me think about what I can do for your friend. Let's meet up at the spring house at eight o'clock in the morning."

"Yes, sir," I said.

Sammie tugged on my sleeve. "Come on. Mama and Buddy will be back soon. I'll walk you home."

"I need to borrow a canteen," I said. "I left mine with Lawrence. Do you have one to spare?"

"Sweetie, get him one from behind the stair railing in the basement."

"Yes, Daddy."

"Don't go upstream along the creek," Hank said once she'd gone. "Men like what you've described will do anything to get what they want. Hopefully, they don't often get downstream this far."

"Yes, Mr. Cordell." I didn't like lying to him.

Sammie returned with a full canteen. Once I'd placed it in my haversack, we went out. The screen door slammed shut behind us.

"Sammie," Hank said from within, "You know better than that."

"Yes, Daddy. I'm sorry."

Outside, the lightning bugs flashed their magic lights. The humidity lower than usual, the night had brought on cooler temperatures and a light breeze. The insects sang and the moon peeked out from behind dark clouds.

I worried about getting Lawrence up the crevice I'd climbed down. That would be especially difficult with a rigid stretcher.

As if reading my thoughts, Sammie said, "Daddy served in the Veterinary Corp in Belgium during the Great War. He'll figure out how to get your friend out."

I nodded and started for the spring house.

"Hey, you're going the wrong way," she said.

"I have to get back to Lawrence."

"Daddy said for you to rest."

"He's your daddy, not mine. Lawrence is waiting in the dark, in terrible pain, not knowing when or if I'll return or if those belonging to Rex might find him and hurt him even more."

"Well, putting it like that…" She approached and gave me another peck on the cheek. "I'll go with you."

"No," I said, giving her a fierce look. "If your father finds you missing, he'll give up on Lawrence and search for you instead. Don't gum this up. Let me do what I can."

She stood silently for a time, looking me in the eye. Finally she glanced down, said, "Do you know what's happened with Seth?"

"No," I said, eager for any news about him. "Tell me."

"I don't know anything, myself, just wondered what you might tell me."

I'd been holding my breath. I let it out. "Haven't been home since I left him in Mama's care."

"Oh, yeah, that makes sense."

Sammie rarely made a mistake like that. That she hadn't foreseen my answer told me she couldn't think straight.

Did I have that effect on her? I know she did on me.

"Don't tell your father that I've gone on ahead. I'll leave arrows in the cave passages for him to find. Tell him to follow only the arrows that have a dot right after the end of their tails. And don't tell him until he's ready to go in the cave that I won't meet him at eight o'clock in the morning."

She looked worried. "Okay."

"Bye," I said with a smile—I was thinking about our second kiss, the one on the lips.

Sammie didn't return my smile. "Be careful," she said.

⌐ ⌐ ⌐

On my return trip, I drew at least twenty arrows of the kind I described to Sammie.

At the spot where I'd earlier gotten stuck up against the wooden pipe, I realized Hank would not be able to get through the tight crawl unless I somehow cleared the tunnel. I kicked the pipe apart with my feet. Water poured from the broken wood, ran down the thin passage, and out into the big room. Getting soaked, I followed the stream out to a drop off, where it fell into darkness. Listening at that edge, I heard the water splashing and spattering far below. Hopefully, until whoever used the water needed more, no alarm would be raised.

I found no one in the big room where the saltpeter mining went on. The place seemed bigger without the busy workers. Echoes came louder and the silence in between felt deeper, more lonely. I moved on.

Lawrence greeted me when I arrived and asked, "May I hold the light for moment." His voice sounded weaker than before.

"Sure." I handed him the carbide lamp.

He nearly put out the flame, hugging it to his chest awkwardly. He gazed at the flame, held a hand up to feel the heat, and gave me the most pitiful, yet grateful look.

I told him some of what to expect with Hank coming to help. He didn't have many questions and he didn't complain that a veterinarian would being giving the aid. No doubt, he knew his rescue would be painful.

"Did you sleep any?" I asked.

"Some. A bad dream awoke me. Let me tell you, waking up from a nightmare in a place that's pitch black is almost as bad as the dream itself. I had no footing and a few moments passed before I knew why I lay upon hard stone hurting so much and remembered what happened to me."

"I'm sorry."

"I've known worse," he said. "Thanks for all you've done. You're a good kid."

Though he'd said a nice thing to me, he looked upset.

"Do you have any more of that aspirin? That did help a little, but now I'm really hurting again."

The pain he had and knowing about the pain to come would leave anyone unhappy.

I got out the aspirin and shook two pills out of the bottle.

"How about four of them," he said.

I handed him the whole bottle, then thought better of it. "Maybe you shouldn't take more than four at one time."

"You're probably right."

"Those men mining saltpeter in the big room—what are they planning to do with old-fashioned gunpowder?"

"You know about the Nashville reservoir breaking open in 1912 and the flood that followed?"

"I've heard tell."

"Rex wants to see that happen again. This time, he and his crew will be standing by, ready to loot certain valuable properties near the flooded areas, while those running the city are distracted trying to protect folks."

"Yeah, but black powder? There are better explosives."

"Rex tried to get cordite. He didn't have the right connections and changes in the National Defense Act made for a bunch of roadblocks. He even started making plans to break into an armory to steal some munitions. At some point, he hit upon the idea of using the old Civil War equipment we found in the cave. The gunpowder they've made—quite a lot—is stored in a dry chamber off the big room."

"If we could blow it—"

"Yeah, without blowing ourselves up." He fell silent, looking defeated.

Trying to come up with a plan to set off the explosive, I thought of too many obstacles. For one thing, I didn't know the layout of the cave. I had questions for Lawrence, then remembered what he'd said the day before, "I don't know the passages well enough to help you." Even if I got the chance to set off an explosion, I feared I wouldn't know how to get out of the cave quickly enough to survive the blast. I couldn't quite remember the route back to the entrance to the cave that I'd originally used when chased by Shufflewell and his men. And that way involved a lot of climbing. The route I felt confident about, the one to the spring house, would be too far to go.

"And this is all done to try and find something called the Will'ven't Bin, right?" I asked.

"You don't believe that tripe, do you?"

"I don't know. Sure seems others do, though."

"Boy howdy, they believe. This place is overrun with such fools.

Rex shows all the new recruits how he can levitate someone and explains that he does that using something called a Li anti-gravity device he bought off a traveling tinker who told him he got the thing from the Will'ven't Bin."

Lawrence suffered a coughing spell before continuing. "A friend of mine, Chip, a naval radio operator during the war, told me that Rex's anti-gravity device looks a lot like his grandmother's hearing aid that she wears in her hairdo. What I saw was a small box with a cord that ran to his ear and another cord running to a hand-held wand that he waved over whoever he levitated. Chip said the cord running to Rex's ear had a tiny speaker in it, the wand was a microphone, and the box was the amplifier. Not long after he told me all that, Chip disappeared. I don't know what happened to him."

The aspirin had done him some good, if his willingness to talk was any sign. What he'd said sounded crazy. I didn't know some of the words he'd used. Not wanting him to think me stupid, I didn't question him.

Instead, to imagine the anti-gravity device, I turned to memories of H. G. Wells's novel *The First Men in the Moon*. In it, a substance called Cavorite is used to nullify gravity. I'd assumed that to be fiction and now had to wonder if I'd been wrong about that.

"Rex tells us the tinker was unclear about where exactly the Bin is," Lawrence said, "but that it's somewhere near here. I swear the levitation looks real, and I believed his story until one of the women, Harriet Whitney, while drunk, told me about Rex's history. She said he'd once earned as a stage magician."

"And 'the turn,'" I said. "What is that?"

"It's merely when everything turns in our favor. The way Rex puts it, once we have the weapons from the Will'ven't Bin, we will not be denied anything. We'll change the country—its politics and laws—in our favor."

"How many followers does he have?"

"He must have at least four-hundred now, and then there are all the officials he's bribed.

"Four-hundred? Where are they all hiding?"

"They're not all are here at the same time. Many are off scavenging or are on other missions in towns nearby."

I didn't know whether or not to believe him.

"Everything we do is a step along the way, Rex says. We raid homes and farms to get food and things to sell. We make gunpowder to blow up the reservoir so we can take more valuables from common folks. He says that what we earn from selling the stuff buys us time to grow our numbers and find the Will'ven't Bin. Once we know where it is, Rex says we'll have such powerful weapons no one will be able to stop us."

"He'd better hurry." I said. "A time will come when his followers will no longer believe him."

"Yeah, well, that hasn't happened yet. From what I can tell, the bigger, more ridiculous the lie, the more his crew carries water for him."

Lawrence grew quiet and seemed to nod off, the pain and his lack of sleep catching up with him, I thought.

Thinking about four hundred men, mostly veterans who had seen war, I remembered the determination of the ants I disturbed on the day Seth pulled hedge stumps. How could I stand up to all the manpower doing Rex's bidding and cleaning up his messes. Not finding any answers, I became fidgety. I wanted to keep moving for fear that Shufflewell and his bullies must surely find us soon.

Lawrence, clearly not sleeping, interrupted my thoughts. "Your Fritz must be the dog Colonel Shufflewell found. He keeps wanting him to be vicious, even though he's not that kind of dog. Sweet pup, your Fritz. I hope you get him back before the Colonel turns him."

"Is he being mistreated?"

"Some. The more frustrated Shufflewell gets, the crueler he is to the dog."

"I'd better hurry, then. We're talking about the man who wears the dirty gray suit, right?"

"Yes."

Lawrence moaned and twisted slightly, trying to get comfortable. "How long before your medic friend gets here?"

"I can't say exactly," I said. "Hank will be here in the morning, maybe at half-past nine o'clock. I don't know what time it is now."

"I wish I could sleep."

"Try to anyway. I want to go take a look at the saltpeter works."

"I was just getting used to having light again," he said sadly.

"This time, I brought another one," I knew I could leave a lamp because Hank would bring it back along with Lawrence.

I got out the extra, the carbide, and the canteen of water Sammie had given me. I filled the hopper and reservoir, and fired the lamp up. Once the light sat beside Lawrence, he gave a big smile.

"I don't know what they might do if they catch you," he said. "Be careful."

"I will."

~ ~ ~

I spent about an hour looking around the big room where the saltpeter mining took place. The men that worked there had nights off, I figured, since the place had gone completely quiet. I located the chamber where they stored twenty-gallon barrels of black powder. Must have been fifty to a hundred of them. Itching to set off all the explosive, I looked for something that might work like a fuse. No luck, I considered opening a barrel and getting out enough powder to lay a trail as a fuse—I'd seen that in a cowboy flick about a gang of villains trying to take control of a silver mine.

Then my thinking changed. I realized how much time it would take to make a trail of powder long enough for me to escape the blast. And what if Fritz were somewhere nearby? What about Hank, Lawrence, and whoever Hank brought along for help? What if big parts of the cave collapsed? No, I could not blow the explosive safely, I decided.

I'd grown weary, and with that, a sleepiness came over me. The time must have been well past midnight. I left the black powder chamber and wandered into another smaller one off the beaten path. The room held several smooth-walled holes in its floor. I turned my lamp off, curled up in one, and closed my eyes, intending to rest for a short time.

~ ~ ~

The sound of a throat clearing awakened me. Looking up, I saw Sammie standing over me, head tilted to one side, left hip thrust out in a cocky stance, and a crooked smile on her face. "You didn't even flinch," she said. "I'm impressed."

Her lamp turned down low, I decided she'd meant to sneak up on me. Wet clothes clung to her awkwardly. She'd probably been soaked coming through the tunnel where I broke the wooden water pipe.

"I followed Daddy and his assistant. They don't know I'm here."

"What time is it?"

"Maybe half-past nine o'clock in the morning," she said, then added, "Saturday morning."

I'd slept through the night!

"Once in the cave, I stopped following them and started looking for you," she said.

"Assistant?"

"Daddy got his Livestock Assistant, Jom Tucklin, to come help."

"Do you think they've gotten to Lawrence yet?"

"Probably. They may be out by now."

"Truly?"

"Yes." she said. "Took me a while to find you. In the meantime, men have begun work in the big room. We should get out of here before someone comes in. If Daddy returns home and I'm not there, he'll come right back out here to look for me. I don't think that's a good thing after hearing what you've said about the people running this place."

"All right."

Skirting the big room to avoid those working, we made our way toward the tunnel that had the broken wooden water pipe. Thinking Hank had rescued Lawrence, I felt myself grow calmer.

I stumbled and Sammie steadied me. Without a word, she took my arm and led me. I knew then that I'd never known such strong feelings for anyone but Sammie. And I also knew that I truly meant something to her. She wanted me safe and was doing her best to keep me that way. Glad tears escaped my eyes. Thankfully, they fell, unseen in the darkness. A wisecrack from Sammie would have spoiled my pleasant thoughts.

"Hey, you," came a female voice from up ahead. "What are you two doing here?"

Lights aimed at our faces blinded me. I turned away and found Sammie's face close by.

"Act like we're local kids spelunking," she whispered.

A man and a woman approached. She looked like the one I thought of as Harriet, the woman Rex's people called Harry. I'd never seen the man before.

"How did you get in here," he asked.

"Through an opening in the hillside," I said.

"Little shit," he said, then backhanded me across the mouth.

I staggered back, my lip split and dripping blood.

Sammie leapt on him and shoved the flame of her carbide lamp in his face. He cried out, pushed her off, and swung a punch at her. She dodged, but he caught her in the gut with another punch.

"No," I cried. I tried to get in there and help. The woman shoved me back.

"Stop, Walter," the woman said. "She's just a girl." She tried to pull the man away.

Sammie stayed down. Walter turned toward me. His angry face had a raw, red burn mark on the right cheek. He felt the wound with his fingers.

I tried to swing an open palm at his left ear. He batted the hand aside and I backed away.

Harry grabbed Sammie by the collar, hauled her up to her feet, and held a knife to her throat. Wide-eyed, she stared at me.

In that moment, I knew they had Sammie. If they took me too, I decided, no one would know what happened to us and I wouldn't have a chance to get her back. Even so, I felt like a cowardly jackass turning and running.

Chapter 16

Completely exhausted and soaking wet from crawling through the tunnel where I'd broken the wooden pipe, I again left the underground through the McClanahan spring house. The sun had climbed almost to noon in the sky.

I didn't return to the Cordells because I feared that if Hank found out that Rex's crew got Sammie, he'd call the police. If he approached one that Rex paid off, that could make our problem worse.

In a deep sinking spell of fatigue, my thinking felt distant and unfinished. I had a hard time juggling my thoughts and plans. Since I didn't know what was happening to Sammie, my brain made up all kinds of horrible suggestions.

Seth might know something that would help, but he'd probably be asleep. Well, I'd just have to wake him up.

Mama would probably be at work. I didn't want to tangle with her. She'd want an explanation of where I'd been and what I'd been up to. I didn't want her to know about Rex and his thugs. If I answered her questions honestly, she'd be the one wanting to go to the police for help.

Tired out, I arrived at my fort, thinking I should lie down and rest again and wait for Seth to awaken.

No, enough dithering. I had to act right away to get Sammie back. I headed through the trees toward the house, figuring I'd tell Mama that, after Sammie and I failed to find Fritz, I had spent the night at the Cordell's house again. Hopefully, she wouldn't question Hank or Marjorie and find out different.

Nearly to the road, I heard the front door of my house open. I ducked behind a webwork of honeysuckle vine and watched. Mama came out. She wasn't dressed for work and didn't carry a lunch sack. That's when I remembered Sammie calling the day Saturday. Mama was off to shop, keep an appointment, or visit someone I reckoned.

She turned her key in the lock on the door and walked off down the street.

The Mama problem solved, I went into the house. Seth, still sleeping, moaned and twisted in the bedding as if having a bad dream. If the nightmare happened to be about the war and I tried to awaken him, would he think me the enemy and lash out?

I uncovered his foot and tugged on his right big toe. The joint of the toe popped and a odd-colored goop oozed from beneath the nail and got on my fingers. I wiped that off on my pants.

"What!" Seth said, his cloudy eyes wide open.

"Rex's people got Sammie."

Seth sat bolt upright. "No!"

"You don't believe me?"

"No. I mean that can't happen."

"Already has. I need your help."

He looked better than I expected.

A car's honking horn drew our attention to the front of the house. I left Seth to go look out a window toward the road. Hank Cordell was getting out of his old, topless Marathon automobile. He approached, and I reluctantly opened the front door for him.

"Where's Sammie?" he asked in a commanding tone.

"I don't know," I tried.

He grabbed me by the shirt and pulled me close. The look in his eyes frightened me. I'd known the man my whole life. He'd never been anything but good to me, so I squashed my panic and said, "If I tell you, you'll want to go to the police for help. You shouldn't do that."

"I'll decide that after I hear what you have to say."

Seth came into the hall and stood waiting to be introduced. He wore some of Daddy's pajamas.

"You must be Seth," Hank said.

Seth nodded and extended a hand.

Hank took it, said, "Sally told me about you and said you'd been injured in the war. I was in Belgium."

Seth moved into the light coming through the door.

Hank's eyes got large and he took a step back. "Is your condition from exposure to mustard gas?"

"Yes."

"Should you be in the hospital?"

"I've been there on and off. They don't have anything for me."

"I'm sorry."

"I'm willing to help. Sammie is your daughter?"

"Yes." Hank turned back to me. "What happened to her?"

"I'm still afraid you'll call the police," I said.

"Would be a mistake to do that," Seth said.

"Tell me!" Hank shouted in my face.

That startled me so much, I fell backwards. I bounced off the doorframe and kept my feet.

At first, telling what happened and how that led to Sammie being taken by Rex's people, I stuttered a lot. Toward the end, though, I had grown confident and outraged. I found myself shouting with angry tears, "You shouldn't have let her follow you, Mr. Cordell. You know what she's like."

"We were in a hurry to get Lawrence out." he said flatly.

"Your daughter is more important than Lawrence," I said. "Strong-willed like she is, she was gonna go with you, even if she had to do it in secret, which is exactly what she did. You're talking to me like all this is my fault, but you're the one who led her inside that cave."

Hank hung his head. "I'm sorry. You love her too, I know. I don't mean to blame you. That's my own guilt looking for an excuse. I need to do something to get her back. I think I'll have to get the police involved."

"If you report this to the wrong policeman," Seth said, "they will make up charges against you and you'll end up in jail. That would delay any efforts to get Sammie back."

Probably thinking about what could be done, Hank looked at Seth for the longest time without saying anything. Finally, he swallowed, rubbed his face and asked, "Why, as sick as you are, do you want to help?"

"Because she's so much like my own daughter, Clara, because Rex killed a friend of mine, and because he is a terrible human being causing a lot of pain among innocent people, many of them his own followers, most of them veterans."

"Okay, thank you."

"I know where they would probably hold her," Seth said, "a pit inside the cave. Those they keep there are lowered down by rope. They cannot climb back up. Certain women are kept there."

By the look on Hank's face, I figured he understood that Sammie was with a bunch of strumpets or other women Rex's crew used.

"If Hank is going to sit there and do nothing," I said to Seth. "Maybe you and I should go get her."

"I'm with you," Seth said.

Hank gave me a sad look. "I'm with you too."

"We'll need rope," Seth said.

"I have that at home," Hank said. He thrust his right hand out to shake Seth's. "Thanks for your help."

Then he turned to me. "And as for you…" He smiled weakly, his eyes sad. "…I'll have to think of a proper way to apologize to you. You just showed me a lot of what your Daddy was made of. Thank you, son."

That warmed my heart.

～ ～ ～

Approaching the Cordell's house, Hank said. "Don't say anything to Marjorie about Sammie. I told her she'd gone to spend the night at the Perry's."

"Okay," I said, while Seth merely nodded.

When we arrived, Hank entered the house all smiles. "Me and the boys have decided to do a Martin Senior-style expedition into a cave,"

He told his wife. "Sorry, no women allowed."

"Even if we were, I wouldn't want to go," she said.

"Where's Buddy?" Hank asked.

"I don't know offhand."

As she caught sight of Seth, she said uncertainly. "Who's your friend?"

"A pal of Daddy's from college," I said, remembering my lie from an earlier evening. "His name is Seth Knopes."

"Nice to meet you, Seth," she said even more uncertainly, her words seeming to come out as a question.

"Likewise, Ma'am. I am recovering from an illness, but please know that I am not contagious."

She nodded and gave him a smile. "Well, let me know if you boys need anything."

"We could use some sandwiches to take with us," Hank said.

"All right," she said, and went into the kitchen.

Buddy came running in through the kitchen door. "I went to your house," he told me. "There's nobody there."

"That's because we're here," I said.

He screwed up a smart-ass smile for me.

Hank took Buddy, Seth, and me outside through the kitchen door and we had a quiet conversation. "Tell Buddy what happened," he told me.

I did. Buddy, listening, became a ball of nervous energy, seeming to struggle to keep himself together and his mouth shut.

"What will they do to her?" he asked when I fell silent.

"We don't know," Hank said. "That's why we're in a hurry."

"We should take the atlatls with us and skewer those bad men," Buddy said.

"We can't do that," Hank said, "and you're staying here. But I need you to know what we're doing."

"No, Daddy, I want to help rescue Sammie."

"I can't risk them taking you too."

Hank turned to me before Buddy could think to say more. "Martin, you know the cave as well as anyone, so I need you and Seth with me. Buddy will stay back at the spring house."

"She's my sister," Buddy wailed. "Martin is just her boyfriend."

Hank's eyes, still on me, grew large.

Not knowing what else to do, I shrugged.

"We'll talk about that later," he said.

That got me worried. What if he thought I wasn't good enough for Sammie?

"I'm going to give you my watch," Hank told Buddy. "The time now is nine o'clock. If we're not back by—" he looked to me. "What do you think, three in the afternoon?"

I looked to Seth for an answer.

"Maybe four would be better," he said.

"—You must stand by and only tell your mother about what we're doing if we don't return by four o'clock in the afternoon."

"You know what she'll do," I said.

"Yes," Hank said, "but at that point there won't be anything else we can do."

Buddy let his head fall forward so his father would see his disappointment.

"I'm sorry, Buddy. You can help by assembling whatever you think we'll need. Put the stuff on the ground by the automobile in the driveway."

"Come with me," Buddy told me. We went in the house and he started handing me things: three canteens and three haversacks, one holding carbide lamps and supplies. From behind the railing that led down to their basement, he took a sixteen-inch-long bayonet in its sheath.

"Daddy got me that for me at the Army/Navy Surplus store for my birthday and told me not to share it with my friends. That's why you've never seen it. The blade isn't sharp. He took a file to the edge. That will just make the steel hurt more when the bayonet goes in."

For such a young fool, the look in his eyes gave me a chill.

"I can't take that," I said. "Too long."

"Isn't for you," he said. He took the weapon into his room and left it behind the door.

I didn't question that, since we were in a hurry. No sense getting him in trouble right before we left.

From a hall closet, he pulled out something in a canvas case.

"Daddy's hunting rifle," he said. "You be careful carrying that to the car. There're boxes of shells inside and the rifle has a scope that's Daddy's pride and joy."

He sounded upset.

"You mean like on a sniper's rifle?"

"A what?" Buddy asked impatiently.

"A sniper is a soldier who can shoot someone from very far away because he has a magnifying scope on his rifle. Seth told me about that."

"Could be," he mumbled.

"Never mind."

Last of all, in the kitchen, we grabbed sacks holding the sandwiches Marjorie had made.

He glanced around as if to see if his mother listened in. I didn't see her. "Mama says they're chicken sandwiches and that she made two for each of us," Buddy said. "Too bad she didn't know about Sammie and Lawrence." He looked annoyed.

"We'll have to share," I said.

We took the sack that held the carbide lamps to the bathroom, cleaned and loaded them with water and carbide, then divvied them and their supplies up between the three haversacks we would take with us. One sack had a growing wet spot on the bottom.

"Yours will be the one with the leaky canteen," he said coldly.

"*What?*" I asked. "Why are you acting that way with me?" We'd walked back outside.

"You haven't told Daddy I should come with you," he whispered.

I didn't know what to say. I thought Hank was right to say no to him. Surprised me that he allowed *me* to come on the expedition.

Grumbling beneath his breath, Buddy turned suddenly and

marched back into the house.

Hank and Seth helped me load everything into the car. We got in, drove toward the McClanahan place, parked down the hill from the mansion near the creek, and walked to the spring house, carrying our divvied-up burden.

~ ~ ~

Seth led us deep inside the cave, to parts I had not yet seen. About an hour in, he said, "We're close to the pit where they keep the women, so keep your voices low."

We came out of a tunnel into a room that had a deep, smooth-sided pit in the floor like a giant bowl. Gathering at the edge, we shone our lamps downward. At least fifty feet deep, the pit would be perfect for holding prisoners, but there wasn't anyone there.

"Damn," Seth said.

"Yeah," Hank agreed.

"We'll have to look around," I said.

Hank nodded.

"Follow me," Seth said.

We walked around the bowl and entered another tunnel. Coming upon a Y-shaped fork in out path, Seth wasn't quite sure which way to go.

"I could go one way, Hank could go the other, and you could stay back to relay messages." I suggested.

"No," Hank said. "Sally would kill me if I lost you."

"You're not going to lose me."

"There are too many dangers."

"Hank's right," Seth said.

He chose the left-hand passage. Moving forward, he shared more doubts that we headed the right way.

Following in the rear, I had an idea. I waited until we were in a tight space—tighter for them than me. "Stay here and I'll check the other branch," I said.

"No," Hank said.

I turned quickly and fled back the way we'd come. He reached for me and missed. I moved so fast, I smacked my head against overhanging formations twice.

"You come back this instant, young man."

I ignored him. I couldn't hear what Seth said clearly, but he seemed to be reassuring Hank.

I got to the fork and went into the unexplored passage. The tunnel narrowed until I had to wriggle on my belly to go forward, my carbide lamp held in my left hand. The light jerked about as I moved. At the end, beyond a hole almost too small to get through, the cave opened up into a larger room. I thought I saw a flash of light in that space, then decided my imagination had gotten the better of me.

At the hole, trying to poke my way through, something or someone grabbed me. Jerked roughly, I popped free into the larger room and fell head first onto the stone floor.

Chapter 17

Some of what followed that day is a mystery to me. At first, since my head had been rung like bell, I had a terrible headache and couldn't make heads nor tails of what was happening. A jumble of gripping hands, jostling arms, and glaring faces dragged me roughly through several cave passages until we came to an opening that let out into daylight.

That light brought my senses back slowly. I hadn't seen that entrance to the cave before.

And, finally, I could count those dragging me along: six men, four in full or partial uniforms of different regiments and ranks, one in rags, another wearing overalls and a straw hat.

They dragged me along a muddy path that became a road with ruts from wagon wheels and automobile tires. The ruts held water from recent rains. Puddles appeared here and there all over the ground, and I realized that there must have been rain in the night.

The dirt road led straight into a cluster of numerous shacks that I recognized as Rex's makeshift community. Men, many in old, ratty military uniforms, came out of the shacks to watch us go by. One of them spit a long string of brown tobacco juice onto my left shoe. Another looked me in the eye, said, "You're gonna die." Most showed little emotion. Some chuckled and others scowled.

My senses mostly restored, I looked around. Like I recalled from my last visit, the shacks stood about ten feet apart, in rings around a central crossroads with an island in the middle that held two wicker chairs. At a glance, though I saw figures seated in them, I could not make out who they might be. Paths led to the doorways of each shack. I say paths, but they were simply tracks where foot traffic had discouraged weeds from growing. Rubbish lay in drifts here and there: Cans, bottles, paper, torn and stained clothing, a few pieces of broken furniture, a cracked door, and a smashed window sash. Smoke drifted upward from what must have been several cook fires. I thought I heard a steam turbine somewhere in the distance. Having seen the community from up in a tree just days earlier helped me understand what I saw much better.

We headed toward the crossroads. Getting closer, I saw that Rex sat in one of the wicker chairs. Someone much smaller sat in the other one, gesturing at the Englishman in an insulting manner. With that, I recognized Sammie.

I wanted to run to her and do whatever I could to get her out of there, but I knew I'd be stopped. Several men with rifles stood behind the wicker chairs. The closer we got to the center, the more I saw our situation as hopeless. Rex's followers kept coming out of the shacks to watch us, their numbers too many to count. Many had firearms, rifles, pistols, and shotguns. A small army had us surrounded. Ragtag though they might have been, they still had me so frightened, I couldn't see any possibility of escape.

"This blowhard thinks he's something," Sammie told me when I got close. "He's spent every moment with me bragging about himself. I've never met such a sad, little man."

She had a bloodied forehead and a bruise on her left cheek.

"Are you okay?" I asked.

Sammie nodded. I felt some relief.

"She's fine," Rex said in his queer accent. "Can't you tell by that nasty mouth of hers?"

"Why did you hurt her?"

"Harry did that, not me. I won't harm her if I can help it." He lit a pipe and slouched in his chair, puffing blue smoke that smelled sweet. "You're not alone, are you?"

"Yes," I said. "She and I are spelunkers, just trying to have some fun. We don't mean any harm."

Rex looked at me for a long time, then a smile grew on his face. "I learned that American's are harder to read when they lie. Something about not having nobles here and feeling like you're in charge of your own world makes you better at concealing the truth. Now, though, I've been here long enough that I can read your 'tells.' I know you're lying."

"No you don't," I said with all the confidence I could muster. "We're kids out having fun. You should let us go home. Our parents are expecting us."

He raised one eyebrow, yet I saw a small doubt.

By now the roads and paths closest to us had filled with people, mostly men. Rex seemed to have few female followers. The overlapping murmur of voices kept me from understanding anything any one of them might have said. Many of them glared at me and Sammie, some gestured rudely.

"Aren't you the kid that was here a couple days ago, climbing around in the trees?" Rex asked.

Although I stood within ten feet of him, he spoke loudly, as if his words were truly meant for those surrounding us. His followers seemed to hang on his every word, those in the distance cupping their ears with hands to hear better.

"I've never been here until today," I said.

"Again with the lies..." He adjusted his bowler hat and pulled at the arm openings of his threadbare waistcoat—the cloth must have been cutting into the fat of his armpits. Big rings of sweat had formed under his arms.

"When younger," Rex said, "I was given to believe that if I behaved well and made myself presentable to the upper classes, my expectations would be good. But being one with little pocket money, I found few avenues open to me. Born into nobility, it seemed I could easily have come from a low-class family. I got into trouble with debt."

He reached for a bottle of amber liquid next to his right foot and took a drink.

"After I came to America, I learned that the most successful people—your country's aristocrats—got where they are through lying, cheating, and stealing. Fraud and abuse of the common man, it appeared, were the preferred methods by which they got rich. Only 'suckers' behave themselves. Well, I know how to be dishonest. Now, I'm using that ability to help these people gain something of their own, all while carving out a little kingdom for myself. Why be good if you can be rich instead?"

A cheer went up from those surrounding us, with lots of whooping and hollering.

"You're a true man of the people," I said sarcastically.

He turned an angry face toward me. I didn't have enough sense to be afraid. I'd become miserable, standing in the hot sun, my head pounding from the blow to my noggin. And I'd grown angry.

"What about the common good?" I asked. Daddy had taught me about that and the need to abide by the law.

"The common good is for rubes."

"What's a rube," I asked.

"Just another word for sucker."

The sound of a gun shot came from the southwest.

"No peace for the wicked," Rex said. "Platoon one, investigate that."

Maybe thirty men broke away to go toward the southwest.

"Colonel!" he shouted.

"He's gone to the privy," someone said. "His favorite is up by the cave entrance."

"Go get him," Rex commanded.

"Yes, sir." That someone trotted off toward the cave.

Rex continued his pontificating until Colonel Shufflewell appeared, making his way toward us from the hills to the north along the same path I'd just taken. My heart did a flip as I saw him leading Fritz. The dog yanked on his leash, choked, and whined. Nobody seemed to notice him looking at me the whole time.

Shufflewell kicked Fritz hard in the rump. The dog yelped, then swung around to bite him, seemed to think better of it, and merely growled, crouching slightly and tucking his tail between his legs. I wanted to go to him, yet, again, I figured Rex would have me stopped, and they might beat me.

Another gun shot, this time from the south. I scanned the horizon, my gaze coming to rest on a tree to the west. I'm certain that was the one I climbed the day I found Rex's community.

As I watched, what looked like a bundle of sticks fell out of that tree, followed by a small person. The person bent and picked up two of the sticks, a thick one and a thin one.

In that small action, I recognized Buddy, the atlatl, and spears. No one appeared to be near him. All eyes seemed to be on Rex and me except for those trying to find the shooter toward the south.

Another gun shot from the Southwest. This time, the bullet struck the back of Rex's wicker chair.

He bolted from his seat and hid behind the one that held Sammie. "Platoon two, go!" Rex shouted. "Get that shooter."

At least half the remaining men watching us broke away to go toward the Southwest.

I looked toward the west, saw Buddy had loaded a spear into his atlatl. He ducked into bushes and became much harder to see.

Shufflewell, much nearer now, still struggled to control Fritz.

"Come here, boy," Rex said to me.

"No," I said.

He grabbed Sammie's hair and jerked her up onto her feet.

She screamed.

A bullet coming from the south struck the ground near Rex's right foot, which stuck out from behind Sammie's chair. He gasped, let go of Sammie, and pulled his leg back behind the wicker, as if that would protect him. A fearful look took hold of his face.

A man in an army private's uniform stepped forward to help shield Rex. A bullet struck his foot and he collapsed. Blood welled up out of the hole in his shoe as he rolled on the ground screaming.

"The rest of you, go get him!" Rex bellowed, pointing southwest.

All but two women headed in that direction.

"What's wrong, Rex," I asked. "You don't have a gun, so you have to hide behind a little girl?"

"I don't need one. My followers give me power."

"Who are you calling a 'little girl?'" Sammie asked me with a sly smile.

Seeing Rex scared gave me courage. I approached him. The two women moved toward me. They didn't look threatening, so I ran at them. They turned and fled, squealing.

Feeling overly confident, I made the mistake of going back toward Rex. When I got close enough, he grabbed me by the hair and slung me to the ground. Landing on my left shoulder, I cried out, and rolled away from him before getting to my feet.

Rex grabbed Sammie by the hair again, turned her toward him and slugged her in the face. She screamed again and wriggled in his grip.

"She'll get more of that if you persist," he said.

"Stop it," he shouted at her.

She wriggled harder.

The man with the hole in his foot, eying me angrily, tried to get up. Another gun shot caught him in the hip and down he went again.

"Whoever that is," I said, "he's a crack shot."

Rex's eyes got large. Sammie crouched suddenly, forced a sharp elbow into his crotch. He let go of her. I grabbed Sammie's hand and pulled her away toward the entrance to the cave in the north.

Glancing about as we ran, I saw Buddy throw a spear with the at-latl. Both Sammie and I stopped to watch.

The spear raced through the air in a long arc, pierced Rex's lower left leg, and pinned him to the ground. His hands went wide, his pipe went flying, and his eyes bulged. He stared in horror at the shaft that had gone through his leg. Finally, struggling to pull the spear out of the ground and his leg, he screamed. That seemed to hurt him so much, he quit trying and lay on the ground panting, tears streaming down his face, his pinned leg in an awkward position. Now that I could see up his pant's leg past his sock, I saw that the stone point and shaft had gone through between the two bones of his lower leg. Blood welled up, soaking his sock.

Sammie gave me a wide-eyed look and a smile.

I didn't have time to smile back. Shufflewell had caught up with us. He raised a pistol to fire at me. I crouched. Much smarter, Sammie broke off to my right, running. I cringed, expecting a bullet to pierce my flesh any moment.

Fritz's jerking movement spoiled Shufflewell's aim. He kicked the dog, and raised the pistol again. I thought surely I was a goner, but Fritz spun and bit what he could reach of the man: the arm holding the pistol. He held on, growling, shaking the arm, his teeth opening angry wounds. Colonel Shufflewell's knees buckled and he went down screaming. The pistol fell from his hand, hit the hard-packed dirt, and went off, the bullet striking him in the right leg.

Gertie appeared out of nowhere. She grabbed Shufflewell's neck in her giant teeth and shook him like a rag doll.

Hurrying over to pick up the pistol, I had to jump out of Gertie's and Fritz's way. Growling, they tugged Shufflewell in opposite directions, slowly spinning clockwise. The man didn't complain, even as they tore new holes in his flesh. That told me I didn't need to be concern about him anymore.

A roar came from behind me and I turned to see Seth running in our direction, maybe a hundred men following him. He looked at something small held in his hands, and pushed on it with his thumbs. That reminded me of what I'd seen him do to the green, fish-shaped piece of flint when he'd gotten its rectangles to line up.

"Run away," Seth shouted. "They're coming right now."

And we did run. I heard rapid gun fire. Glancing back, I saw men in uniform in the distance coming our way, an army of them. They held rifles at the ready and fired on Rex's men. I recognized the sound of mortar fire, saw explosions marching toward the island in the middle of the community. Then I heard a deeper booming in the distance that I thought might be artillery fire. Screaming projectiles came racing toward us, ending in explosions that tore our enemies apart while leaving us whole. One went off within a few feet of Seth and he walked out of the blast unharmed.

A yellowish brown gas flowed out from behind him as he ran. Some of the men chasing him entered the cloud. Others backed off, in a panic to avoid the stuff.

I had to wonder if I'd just witnessed a mustard gas attack. If so, how had Seth made that happened?

Those that had backed off, now rallied and started around the cloud.

Seth stopped, turned around, and began to rise up into the air. Hovering about ten feet off the ground, he raised his hands towards those chasing him. Flame seemed to spew forth from his palms, setting them ablaze. Wherever the stuff fell, the burning continued with bright flames, even in puddles of water. Screams of agony discouraged those still on their feet. A few broke away and ran in the opposite direction.

Impossible!

My mind reeled, yet I could only witness the madness and move on, since I couldn't understand what was happening.

And now, I could see the soldiers Seth had conjured more clearly—some wore French uniforms, some wore British or American ones. A few uniforms I'd never seen before. Some of the black soldiers wore turbans. I even saw a few in the German gray with the pointy helmet. They all fired on Rex's men, and left us alone.

Injured or dead, men fell, having been shot by the approaching army.

The dogs had given up on Shufflewell and run on ahead of us. Fritz looked back. When he saw Sammie and me running, he kept going.

His feet back on solid ground, Seth turned onto one of the intersecting paths and headed north toward the entrance to the cave. Now we headed in roughly the same direction, about fifty yards apart. The men belonging to Rex chased Seth, several firing pistols or rifles. He appeared to be struck a couple of times, but kept running without pause.

A few of Rex's men gathered to chase Sammie and me. Seeing that, Seth raised his right hand as if it were a pistol. He looked for all the world like a child playing cowboys and Indians, silently mouthing a word—probably "bang"—several times. For each "bang" I heard a gun shot that seemed to come from his pointing index finger. Glancing back, I saw a man chasing us fall, like he'd truly been shot. After the sound of several more shots close by, I looked back again and saw that all of those that had been chasing us now lay dead or badly wounded upon the ground.

Headed uphill toward the cave, I thought about all the men working there. I shouted to Seth, "Don't go to the cave. It's full of Rex's men."

"I must," he shouted back. "The black powder. You two go back. Run away as fast as you can."

I came to a stop, and Sammie ran into me. We landed on the ground in a heap.

The dogs stopped and came back for us. Thankfully, Fritz didn't choose that moment for a reunion. Even a grateful tongue would have been in the way. I had to get to my feet quickly.

Standing and helping Sammie up, I could see the cave entrance up the hill. The last I saw of Seth, he'd begun to glow as he entered the darkness.

"We have to get far away from the cave," I said.

We got up and ran, giving everything we had. The dogs too. I stumbled and fell, skinning my knees and forearms. Sammie helped me up and we ran again.

Ahead of us, I saw Buddy running toward the island in the middle of the community. The wicker chairs lay upset on their sides, one burning. Rex still lay where the spear had pinned him. Buddy approached the man, reached into his haversack, and pulled out the bayonet. He removed and dropped the sheath.

"No," I shouted, but he didn't hear me.

Buddy knelt beside Rex, raised the bayonet to stab the Englishman, and stopped.

Nearly to them, I saw that Rex's upper body and head had been severely burned, and that he had died of his wounds.

We came to a stop next to Buddy.

"Damn it," he said.

"A good thing he's gone." I said, panting and choking on spit I'd inhaled.

"I wanted to do that for Sammie," Buddy said.

Sammie's bruised face smiled. "You put a spear through him for me. That's even better." She grabbed and hugged him tight. "I take back all the nasty things I've said about you. You are the best brother in the world."

"We've got to get out of here," I said, trying to pull Sammie away.

They let go of one another and we all ran, dodging things or jumping over them in order to keep a straight route away from the cave.

Getting a dizzy feeling, I realized that a quaking in the ground left my footing uncertain. I looked back toward the hill that held the cave entrance, saw trees sway and shake. Then the hill seemed to slump and a great roar went up along with a column of smoke and dust.

What remained of Rex's people scattered.

Epilogue

As I write this at the age of twenty-five, I can't say I have a better understanding of what I call the Battle of Brown's Creek than I had at age twelve. The mysteries of that summer haunt me still.

After the battle in August of 1933, stunned to silence, Sammie, Buddy, and I walked away from what remained of Rex's community to make our way home. Gertie and Fritz took us to Hank. He sat in the weeds, unharmed except for a deep cut on his forearm that Sammie fussed over, even though he told her to leave him be.

"That son of a bitch cut me with his knife," he said, sounding angry. He pointed to a man that lay insensible in the brush nearby. "I bashed his face with the butt of my rifle."

Hank fell silent as a sadness seemed to come over him. He lay back and closed his eyes.

Fritz and I had our reunion. While he got lots of petting, I got a wet face from that grateful tongue of his. I didn't mind, though his mouth smelled like he'd been eating poo. Shufflewell probably hadn't fed him well.

Hank rose and directed us with gestures. We gathered up our stuff and walked home along Brown's Creek. The dogs, knowing where we headed, ran ahead of us, only to circle back a lot to see if we still followed.

We didn't speak for the longest time. I figured everyone had been troubled by the death and destruction. Some of what I'd seen, I knew, would keep me up at night. I wondered if Sammie and Buddy would suffer the same. Were we likely to get the sickness of the head that troubled Seth and the Cordell children's cousin, Harold Timmons?

I knew no good would come from worrying about that.

Finally, Hank said, "You're not to talk about what happened—none of you—do you hear me?"

"Why, Daddy?" Sammie asked.

"We used weapons against other human beings and..." A tear slid down his cheek. "...and at least one that I shot died. I didn't mean for that to happen. I've never killed anyone before, not even in the fight in Belgium."

Sammie and I nodded, understanding his sadness.

Buddy gave arguments for why the killing had been reasonable.

"No," Hank said. "Do you hear me, son? You will tell no one, not a single person."

"Yes, Daddy."

Buddy said little more all the way home.

~ ~ ~

Mama grounded me for a month.

"You're treating me like an airplane with a mechanical problem," I told her.

"Is that where the expression, 'grounding,' comes from?" she asked.

"Probably."

"Well, maybe that's just what you are, young man, a broken airplane that wants to soar, but flies too high and keeps getting into trouble."

Mama had never called me a "young man" before.

She made a pallet of old quilts to put in my room for Fritz to sleep on and told me he had permission to stay nights with me anytime I wanted. Also, she let Sammie and Buddy visit during my grounding.

We whiled away what remained of the summer playing a lot of cards, mostly Eights. Buddy brought over the plans for our next electrical tower, and we built that one from flat toothpicks in my room on Mama's card table, the one she used when she and her friends played bridge.

"What if we get glue on it?" I asked.

"You can put newspaper down," Mama said. "But if you still get some on it, wipe the surface smooth before it dries. I have a small tablecloth that will hide any blemishes."

I welcomed the change in her, suspecting it had something to do with stuff Hank might have told her about what we'd all been up to. I knew they'd had a conversation because I saw them standing on the road out front of the house where she'd parked the automobile—a Ford with a rumble seat—she'd bought from Olin Turner. The serious looks on their faces and the grimaces Mama made told me they weren't just talking about the care and maintenance of the contraption. As soon as they saw me approaching, they suddenly and awkwardly quit speaking and began a new subject that seemed out of the blue.

That afternoon, Hank and I finished clearing of the hedge stumps where the driveway would enter our yard. We dug up the rest of the roots, used dirt from the northwest corner of our lot to fill the holes, then spread sulfuric acid on the strip of ground where the entire driveway would be when finished. The acid killed the weeds, and a week later when the truck of gravel arrived, the ground was ready. Mama grinned ear to ear as she drove her automobile into the driveway for the first time.

~ ~ ~

What Sammie and Buddy remembered of the day we brought down Rex and his crew turned out to be very different from my recollections. Whenever I talked about what I saw and did, they looked at me like I'd gone mad.

They had not seen or heard the WWI soldiers. They did not recall seeing the cloud of yellow-brown gas, the liquid fire, the bullets coming from Seth's hand, or him glowing and levitating.

"You're making all that up," Buddy said.

"How do you think we got away from those people?" I asked. "There were hundreds of them."

"I don't know," Sammie said. "Daddy is awfully sharp with that rifle of his."

"Yeah," Buddy said, "I figured he scared them witless."

Did they play dumb on purpose?

"What happened to Seth?" I asked.

They both looked downcast at that.

"He was the real hero," Sammie said, "Running into the cave and giving his own life to blow up the black powder."

Buddy nodded agreement with his sister.

On September first, Hank came to the house to bring me the carbide lamp I'd left with Lawrence. I asked what he remembered of that terrible day. "We're not going to discuss that," he said. From the look in his eyes, I knew to drop the subject.

Still, I needed to know I hadn't merely been seeing things. I'd been looking about for word of the events at Rex's place and the cave. The Banner, a conservative newspaper, had no mention of those happenings at all. The Tennessean, a liberal newspaper, referred to the abandoned place as a "negro hobo camp," saying that the police had cleared out an ugly and menacing community. Neither paper said anything about a cave or an explosion.

One day, while the three of us played cards, I mentioned that Seth had shot some of Rex's people with his finger. I'd held that back for the longest time because when I practiced in my head putting those memories into words, they seemed awfully silly and unbelievable.

Laughing, Sammie said, "Show me what that looked like."

I felt foolish holding up my index finger and saying "bang."

Even as they enjoyed great belly laughs at that, I had aimed out the open window for fear that something in the house might get damaged if a bullet actually fired from my finger. With Hank's unwillingness to talk about the events and knowing I'd never be able to persuade Sammie and Buddy that what I described really happened, I felt a frustration that took months to wear off. Truth is, even now that I'm in college at Vanderbilt University, I suffer moments of annoyance over all that.

I got the notion that the Will'ven't Bin had indeed been real, that Seth found its location, and somehow absorbed some of the inventions. Even if that were true, though, I don't know when he might have done that and I couldn't have said how that explained any of what happened.

Had Seth released a cloud of mustard gas? Did that come from what he'd absorbed during the war? Had Greek fire spewed from his hands? Did he indeed levitate and shoot bullets from his finger? Had the pain of his experience during the war become a weapon he used against Rex and his people? Was the green, fish-shaped piece of flint actually some sort of time machine that allowed him to call upon the war to come to his aid? Even though those questions have no answers, by my reckoning Seth had performed the impossible.

Hank, Sammie, Buddy and I all assumed he had died in the explosion or cave-in. Although he'd suffered the loss of much of what he loved, he had sacrificed everything to defend life.

And yet, he lived on in memory. So much so that for the longest time I couldn't shake the feeling that he'd knock on our door one day and ask for work. When I pictured that in my mind, I couldn't help seeing his daughter too. She stood next to him on our stoop, her mop of curly brown hair hanging down over one eye.

Like Mama, I'm not much of a believer, but if there is something good beyond this life, I hope Seth joined his Clara there.

My own sense of loss began to fall away, replaced with the knowledge that Daddy had not left me behind. His visits could be found in my thoughts and interests, my curiosity and bearing. As I grew older, more and more frequently I would find him in the mirror as well.

~ ~ ~

One day Sammie showed up alone.

"Where's Buddy?" I asked.

"I can't teach you with him around."

"Teach me what?"

"A brand new verb, smooching."

"What does it mean?"

"I'll explain by teaching you how."

Mama at work, we had the house to ourselves. The lessons went on all afternoon.

~ ~ ~

Once I'd been freed from my grounding, Buddy, Sammie, and I walked up Brown's Creek, past the fishing camp, to the remains of Rex's community. The place had been abandoned and machinery had chewed up the ground. Most of the shacks had been bulldozed away. The prints of bulldozer tracks and those of mule-drawn wagons were everywhere in the mud. Except for the sounds of birds and insects, the place had gone quiet. Soon, the weeds and brush would swallow the trash, the roads, and paths and there would be nothing left to tell the tale of Rex, his crew, and their plot.

They had intended to take over the government, but a wounded veteran, a man with a hunting rifle, and little boy with an atlatl stopped them.

End

Author, illustrator, and publisher, Alan M. Clark, grew up in Tennessee in a house full of bones and old medical books. In his forty years as a freelance illustrator, he has created illustrations for hundreds of books, including works of fiction of various genres, nonfiction, textbooks, young adult fiction, and children's books. During his thirty years as a freelance writer, he has authored twenty-three published books, including seventeen novels, a lavishly illustrated novella, a lavishly illustrated novelette, four collections of fiction, and a nonfiction full-color book of his artwork. Honors for his work include the World Fantasy Award, four Chesley Awards, and he is an International Book Awards winner. Alan M. Clark and his wife, Melody, live in Oregon.

www.alanmclark.com

IFD Publishing Paperbacks

Novels:

Of Thimble and Threat, by Alan M. Clark
Baggage Check, by Elizabeth Engstrom
Bull's Labyrinth, by Eric Witchey
The Surgeon's Mate: A Dismemoir, by Alan M. Clark
Siren Promised, by Jeremy Robert Johnson and Alan M. Clark
Say Anything but Your Prayers, by Alan M. Clark
Candyland, by Elizabeth Engstrom
Apologies to the Cat's Meat Man, by Alan M. Clark
Lizzie Borden, by Elizabeth Engstrom
A Parliament of Crows, by Alan M. Clark
Lizard Wine, by Elizabeth Engstrom
The Door that Faced West, by Alan M. Clark
The Northwoods Chronicles, by Elizabeth Engstrom
The Prostitute's Price, by Alan M. Clark
The Assassin's Coin, by John Linwood Grant
13 Miller's Court, by Alan M. Clark and John Linwood Grant
Guys Named Bob, by Elizabeth Engstrom
Fallen Giants of the Points, by Alan M. Clark
The Itinerant, by Elizabeth Engstrom
York's Moon, by Elizabeth Engstrom
Night Birds, by Lisa Snellings and Alan M. Clark
The Witch of Wapping, by Rebecca J. Allred and Alan M. Clark
The Will'ven't Bin, by Alan M. Clark

Collections:

Suspicions, by Elizabeth Engstrom
Professor Witchey's Miracle Mood Cure, by Eric Witchey
Unrequited Loss, by Elizabeth Engstrom

Nonfiction:
How to Write a Sizzling Sex Scene, by Elizabeth Engstrom
Divorce by Grand Canyon, by Elizabeth Engstrom

IFD Publishing EBooks
(You can find the following titles at most distribution points for all
ereading platforms.)

Novels:
The Prostitute's Price, by Alan M. Clark
The Assassin's Coin, by John Linwood Grant
13 Miller's Court, by Alan M. Clark and John Linwood Grant
Guys Named Bob, by Elizabeth Engstrom
Apologies to the Cat's Meat Man, by Alan M. Clark
Bull's Labyrinth, by Eric Witchey
The Surgeon's Mate: A Dismemoir, by Alan M. Clark
York's Moon, by Elizabeth Engstrom
Beyond the Serpent's Heart, by Eric Witchey
Lizzie Borden, by Elizabeth Engstrom
A Parliament of Crows, by Alan M. Clark
Lizard Wine, by Elizabeth Engstrom
Northwoods Chronicles, by Elizabeth Engstrom
Siren Promised, by Alan M. Clark and Jeremy Robert Johnson
To Kill a Common Loon, by Mitch Luckett
The Man in the Loon, by Mitch Luckett
Of Thimble and Threat, by Alan M. Clark
Jack the Ripper Victim Series: The Double Event (includes two novels
from the series: *Of Thimble and Threat* and *Say Anything But Your
Prayers*) by Alan M. Clark
Candyland, by Elizabeth Engstrom
The Blood of Father Time: Book 1, The New Cut, by Alan M. Clark,
Stephen C. Merritt & Lorelei Shannon
The Blood of Father Time: Book 2, The Mystic Clan's Grand Plot, by

Alan M. Clark, Stephen C. Merritt & Lorelei Shannon
How I Met My Alien Bitch Lover: Book 1 from the Sunny World Inquisition Daily Letter Archives, by Eric Witchey
Baggage Check, by Elizabeth Engstrom
D.D. Murphry, Secret Policeman, by Alan M. Clark & Elizabeth Massie
Black Leather, by Elizabeth Engstrom
Fallen Giants of the Points, by Alan M. Clark
The Itinerant, by Elizabeth Engstrom
Night Birds, by Lisa Snellings and Alan M. Clark
The Witch of Wapping, by Rebecca J. Allred and Alan M. Clark
The Will'ven't Bin, by Alan M. Clark

Novelettes:
Mudlarks and the Silent Highwayman, by Alan M. Clark
The Tao of Flynn, by Eric Witchey
To Build a Boat, Listen to Trees, by Eric Witchey

Children's Illustrated:
The Christmas Thingy, by F. Paul Wilson. Illustrated by Alan M. Clark

Collections:
Suspicions, by Elizabeth Engstrom
Professor Witchey's Miracle Mood Cure, by Eric Witchey
Unrequited Loss, by Elizabeth Engstrom

Short Fiction:
"Brittle Bones and Old Rope," by Alan M. Clark
"Crosley," by Elizabeth Engstrom
"The Apple Sniper," by Eric Witchey

Nonfiction:
How to Write a Sizzling Sex Scene, by Elizabeth Engstrom
Divorce by Grand Canyon, by Elizabeth Engstrom

IFD Publishing Audio Books

Novels:

The Door That Faced West by Alan M. Clark, read by Charles Hinckley

Jack the Ripper Victim Series: Of Thimble and Threat, by Alan M. Clark, read by Alicia Rose

Jack the Ripper Victim Series: Say Anything But Your Prayers, by Alan M. Clark, read by Alicia Rose

Jack the Ripper Victim Series: The Double Event, by Alan M. Clark, read by Alicia Rose (includes two novels from the series: *Of Thimble and Threat* and *Say Anything But Your Prayers*)

A Parliament of Crows, by Alan M. Clark, read by Laura Jennings

A Brutal Chill in August, by Alan M. Clark, read by Alicia Rose

The Surgeon's Mate: A Dismemoir, by Alan M. Clark, read by Alan M. Clark

Apologies to the Cat's Meat Man, by Alan M. Clark, read by Alicia Rose

The Prostitute's Price, by Alan M. Clark, read by Alicia Rose

The Assassin's Coin, by John Linwood Grant, read by Alicia Rose

13 Miller's Court, by Alan M. Clark and John Linwood Grant, read by Alicia Rose

Fallen Giants of the Points, by Alan M. Clark, read by Carolina Cioara

Novelettes:

Mudlarks and the Silent Highwayman, by Alan M. Clark, read by Alicia Rose